A NANNY FOR THE RECLUSIVE
BILLIONAIRE

A NANNY FOR THE RECLUSIVE
BILLIONAIRE

REGINA KYLE

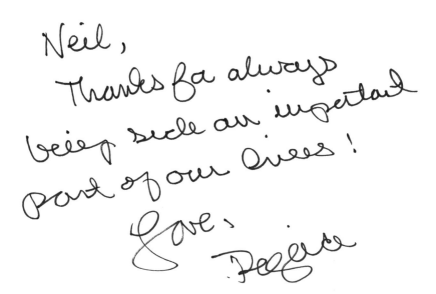

Neil,
Thanks for always
being such an important
part of our lives!
Love,
Regina

Entangled Publishing, LLC
2614 South Timberline Road
Suite 105, PMB 159
Fort Collins, CO 80525
rights@entangledpublishing.com

Indulgence is an imprint of Entangled Publishing, LLC.

Edited by Candace Havens
Cover design by Heather Howland
Cover photography by Justin Horrocks/Getty Images

Manufactured in the United States of America

First Edition September 2018

Chapter One

Mallory Worthington wiped a bead of sweat from her forehead and tied her quarter-zip pullover around her waist. Why hadn't anyone warned her how humid Miami was in June? If she'd known, she would have at least put her hair up so it was off her neck. And traded the jeans and baby-blue suede Pumas for khaki capris and a cute pair of Kate Spade sandals, which would have had the added benefit of showing off her new pedicure, a shimmery beige-pink with the strangely prophetic name Cozu-melted in the Sun.

She hoisted her weekender tote over her shoulder and scanned the sidewalk for the car that was supposed to be waiting to take her the two-plus hours to Rhys Dalton's remote estate in the Florida Keys. The guy owned his own island. How much more reclusive could you get?

Finally, she spotted a distinguished-looking man with graying dark hair standing next to a Lincoln Town Car and holding a sign that read WORTHINGTON in bold bloodred script.

"Miss Worthington?" he asked as she approached.

"Yes." She extended her free hand, but he ignored it and reached for her bag instead.

"Is this all your luggage?"

"Yes." Much more of this and she'd sound like a broken record. She raised herself up to her full height—an unimpressive five-feet-even, thanks to multiple rounds of chemo and radiation that had stunted her growth. Normally she wore at least three-inch heels to compensate, but she'd left most of them at home. She might have learned to work the dining room in stilettos on the rare occasions she turned control of the kitchen over to her sous chef—it was good for morale and helped bridge the gap between front and back of house, and she liked seeing the smiles on the customers' faces—but they wouldn't be much good for chasing an active toddler. "I had most of my things shipped ahead."

She preferred to travel light. Plus, if her things were already down there, she couldn't chicken out at the last minute, could she?

"Right." He popped the trunk and carefully placed her bag inside before slamming it shut. "Mrs. Flannigan has them waiting for you in your quarters."

"Mrs. Flannigan?"

"The housekeeper."

The recruiter had told Mallory she'd be part of a small staff, all living on site. At least she'd have someone to talk to besides her four-year-old charge. Her boss wasn't what anyone would call the chatty type, as she'd learned from their brief phone interview. They'd talked a grand total of maybe five minutes, presumably because the agency had already grilled her to his satisfaction.

"What about you?" she asked the driver. "What's your name?"

"I'm Collins, Mr. Dalton's chauffeur, business manager, and general man-of-all-trades." He held the door open. "If you don't mind, miss. We've got a bit of a drive. I'd like to get moving so we're there before dark."

"No problem." She stepped into the car, a blast of cold from the air conditioner hitting her in the face. "And please, call me Mallory."

"Yes, miss." He closed the door behind her.

Okay then. Miss it was.

Collins—apparently the man had only one name, like Beyoncé or Ludacris—slid behind the wheel and started the engine. Mallory relaxed into the leather seat, her hand landing on a manila folder beside her. "What's this?"

"A little light reading for your trip."

"Light reading?" She picked up the folder.

"A few things you should know before you arrive."

"Like household rules?"

"In a manner of speaking."

That sounded ominous. The whole interview-to-job-offer-to-acceptance process had been so fast, there was a lot about Rhys Dalton she didn't know. He'd needed a nanny ASAP to replace someone who left him in a lurch. Not an ideal job for a Culinary Institute of America–trained chef.

But she had to get out of Dodge before she got cold feet and wound up spending the rest of her life in the looming shadow of her parents and the disease she'd fought and beaten as a child. Even if that meant a temporary career change and putting hundreds of miles between her and her big sister, who'd always been her best friend and moral support.

Brooke had forged a new life for herself—great guy, great job, great apartment—and it was time for Mallory to do the same. That wasn't going to happen if she stayed under her parents' thumb. Working in the family hotel. Living in the family guesthouse. Letting them hover over her like vultures with thermometers, tissues, and Tylenol, waiting for any sign of a sniffle or sneeze.

But in her rush to escape, what had she gotten herself into? What if Rhys Dalton had turned angry and vengeful in his self-imposed seclusion, like Heathcliff in *Wuthering Heights*? Or maybe his wife was still alive, and he had her locked up in his attic, like Mr. Rochester in *Jane Eyre*?

Mallory shook her head. Clearly, she'd been indulging in too much Gothic romance. She'd have to stick to Stephen King from now on. Way less frightening.

The car pulled away from the curb, and she flipped open the folder and began to read. The first few pages were fairly innocuous. Daily schedule. Dietary requirements for Rhys and his son, Oliver. Emergency contact information in the event of a fire, flood, or alien invasion.

Then she got to the juicy part.

Okay, Rhys Dalton didn't have a wife stashed in his attic. He was a widower, which was tragic enough on its own. Even worse, he'd lost his wife to a terrorist attack. Mowed down on a busy Manhattan street with seven other innocent victims going about their daily routine on a crisp fall morning.

She closed the file and let her head fall back against the smooth, cool leather. No wonder he'd cut himself off from the rest of the world. And no wonder Collins wanted to make sure she had a better understanding of their boss before meeting him face-to-face for the first time.

"Collins?" she asked as the chauffeur expertly merged the car onto the highway.

"Yes, miss?"

"How long have you worked for Mr. Dalton?"

"Almost seven years."

"So, you knew him before…" She let her voice trail off, not sure where to go. What was the politically correct way of saying "before his wife was brutally murdered?"

"Yes, miss."

Collins clearly understood what she'd left unsaid, but he

didn't elaborate, and Mallory was happy to let the subject drop. Maybe when—if—she got to know the man a little better, she'd pump him for more information.

It wasn't that she was morbidly curious. It was more like she felt a sort of kinship with Rhys Dalton, even though she was still hours from meeting him. He'd loved and lost, and so had she. Maybe not a biological family member, but the kids she'd shared the chemo ward with were as close as family. And she'd lain in her hospital bed, helpless, as more than one had lost their battle with cancer, taking a little piece of her with them each time.

"I've got cold water up here if you're thirsty," Collins said, interrupting the depressing turn of her thoughts.

"I'm fine, thanks." Mallory tried to suppress a yawn.

"Feel free to close your eyes and get some rest."

"Thanks." She didn't want to admit it, but the stress, heat, and three hours on a plane were catching up to her. She tired more easily than the average twenty-seven-year-old, something she combated with a daily regimen of pills and potions. Yet another constant reminder of the disease that had come close to taking her life. Almost against their will, her eyelids drooped, and she yawned again. "I think I will."

It could have been ten minutes or ten hours later when Collins's not-so-subtle cough woke her.

"Excuse me, miss. We're at the dock."

"Dock?" She sat up and scrambled for her purse. She had a mirror in there somewhere, didn't she? She was afraid to see what she looked like. Probably had hair stuck to her cheek and drool dripping from her chin.

The door swung open, and Collins reached a hand into the car to help her out. "Yes, miss. It's only a short boat ride from here to the island."

She took the chauffeur's hand and stepped out of the car, the crushed shells that made up the parking lot crunching under the soles of her sneakers. The heat and humidity assaulted her, making her already-sweat-stained shirt and wrinkled jeans feel like they weighed a thousand pounds. Changing into more weather-appropriate clothing would be first on the agenda once she hit land. Again.

But the view almost made up for the temporary discomfort. Puffy white clouds floated across a cerulean sky. An almost translucent blue-green ocean, nothing like the murky northern Atlantic waters she was used to, stretched as far as the eye could see. A red-and-white launch bobbed at the end of a long wooden dock, the outline of an island barely visible in the distance.

"Is that it?" she asked, hurrying after Collins across the parking lot and down the dock. "Mr. Dalton's island?"

"Yes." He hefted her bag into the back of the boat and jumped in after it. The man was so quietly efficient she hadn't even noticed him retrieve it from the trunk. "That's Flamingo Key."

She looked from the boat to the dock and back again, gauging the distance between them. Too far for her short legs to handle. Her hesitation must have been written all over her face, because Collins put a foot on the gunnel and held a hand out to her again.

"It's not as hard as it looks," he reassured her. "I won't let you fall."

She held her breath, put her damp palm into his calloused one and stepped off the dock. True to his word, Collins helped her into the launch without incident. Once he had her settled in the back with her bag, he started the engine and cast off, handling the boat as skillfully as he did the Town Car. He'd left "skipper" off his job description. Unless chauffeur included land and sea vehicles.

Mallory sucked the sea air into her lungs like it was authentic New Zealand manuka honey and grabbed the rails to steady herself. Her hair whipped her cheeks, and she closed her eyes against the warm breeze and the light spray the boat kicked up as it cut through the waves. This was why she'd left New York. This sense of freedom. From her parents. From the responsibilities of running a restaurant.

From her cancer.

A too-short ten minutes later, they were back on terra firma, standing in front of an enormous stucco Venetian-style mansion.

"Mr. Dalton is waiting for you in the study."

Mallory put a hand to her hair, even more of a wreck now after the boat ride. "Can I freshen up first?"

"He has a conference call in ten minutes, and he'd like to see you before you meet Oliver."

"Doesn't he want to introduce me to his son?"

"Mr. Dalton is a busy man. Mrs. Flannigan will take care of the introductions."

Too busy for his own son? This guy was sinking lower in Mallory's esteem, any kinship she might have felt fading like a summer tan in October. Okay, he'd lost his wife. Truly tragic. But that meant his son needed him more than ever.

With an increased sense of impending doom, she followed Collins up the massive stone steps to the equally massive wood-and-glass front door. She tried her best to smother her warring emotions, ping-ponging between wanting to make a good first impression on her new boss and wanting to smack him upside the head for putting work before his motherless child.

"After you," Collins said, holding yet another door open for her. "The study is the first door on the left."

Her stomach flip-flopped. "Aren't you coming with me?"

"No, miss." He gestured for her to enter. "Mr. Dalton is expecting you. I have to check the lines on the launch and make sure your room is ready."

Great. She was going into the lion's den alone, with

nothing but good intentions and a wardrobe that made her look like a reject from one of those *Survivor*-style reality TV shows. She stalled on the top step. "You're sure I won't be disturbing him."

"Just knock first and announce yourself." Collins ushered her into the cavernous marble-tiled foyer. "Mrs. Flannigan will come get you when you're done."

"Thanks." She swallowed hard and willed her reluctant feet to move. Nothing. She could see the study door across the foyer. Those few feet might as well have been a thousand miles for all the good it did her.

"Don't worry," Collins said, lowering his voice. "His bark is worse than his bite."

Was it that obvious she needed a pep talk? She did a quick mental tally. Flushed cheeks. Dry mouth. Sweaty palms. Knocking knees. Yep, it was official. She was a basket case, and it showed.

"Thanks," she repeated, trying to sound braver than she looked.

With a nod, he left. Mallory finally got her feet moving, squeaking across the foyer in her sneakers. When she reached the study door, she hitched her pocketbook up on her shoulder, took a shaky breath, and knocked.

"Enter."

She had to stop herself from backing away. Collins wasn't kidding about the barking. She hoped he was right about the bite, too.

She took another deep, unsteady breath in a futile attempt to calm her jangling nerves and cracked the door open. The room was in semidarkness, shades drawn, lit only by a lamp on the impressive mahogany desk that dominated the space. A man stood behind it with his back to her, one hand holding a cell phone to his ear, the other jammed in the pocket of his butt-hugging khakis.

"I'll be with you in a minute," he said, lowering the phone. Good thing, or she would have had no way of knowing whether he was talking to her or the person on the other end of the line. It wasn't like he bothered to do something crazy like actually look at her when he spoke.

She took the opportunity to study him unobserved while he finished his conversation. He was tall—around six feet, she guessed, dwarfing her tiny frame. Inky black curls dusted the collar of his shirt, a shirt that molded his broad shoulders and back as well as his pants showcased his butt. He'd rolled the sleeves to his elbows, revealing tanned forearms with a smattering of fine dark hair.

Holy hotness. If he looked as good from the front as he did from the back...

Stop. Do not pass Go. Do not collect two hundred dollars. Do not think lustful thoughts about your workaholic, criminally-attractive-from-behind new boss.

"I need that report by five," the object of her lust practically spat into the phone. "And tell Mark I want to talk to him as soon as he's back in the office."

He ended the call without so much as a goodbye and tossed the phone onto his desk, turning to face her as he did. Any hope the full-frontal view would quash the dirty daydreams inspired by his backside was immediately dashed. The grainy picture in the file Collins had shared with her didn't come close to doing him justice. Whiskey-brown eyes, framed by almost obscenely long lashes. Patrician nose. Strong jawline. It all added up to a mouthwatering package of male physical perfection.

Why hadn't she bothered to Google him? Then she would have been prepared for the onslaught of his sheer masculine beauty. If you could ever prepare for something as powerful as that. Or run the other way as fast as her short-girl legs would carry her.

"Miss Worthington?" His eyes, dark and appraising, skated over her less-than-impressive curves, leaving her wondering if the final verdict was desire or derision. Not that it mattered, because she was there to take care of his son's needs, not his own. Or hers.

"Mallory," she corrected, her shaky voice betraying the potent cocktail of nervousness and attraction coursing through her system.

"There's been a misunderstanding. I thought you were"—his gaze traveled the length of her body again, the journey ending this time in a scowl—"older."

His words were like a bucket of ice water dumped over her head, effectively dousing any flickers of awareness. Probably—no, definitely—a good thing considering their circumstances. It was practically a cliché, the world-wise billionaire and the innocent, virginal nanny.

"Is that a problem?" she asked sharply. She was twenty-seven, not seventeen. More than mature enough to handle a preschooler. Heck, she'd run a commercial kitchen, managed almost a hundred employees from sixteen to sixty, some of them no better behaved than your average four-year-old. Hadn't he read her résumé?

"I'm afraid so." He jabbed a button on the intercom on his desk. "Mrs. Flannigan, we're ready for you now."

Mallory shook her head, plastering several damp strands against her cheek and no doubt making her look even younger. Not helping her cause one bit. She pushed the sticky strands off her face and straightened, maximizing every inch of her five-foot frame. "I don't understand."

"I'm sorry you've come all this way for nothing." He crossed to the door, his powerful strides eating up the short distance, and opened it. "I'll see you get the earliest possible flight home, and you'll be compensated for your time and trouble."

Chapter Two

Rhys let out a relieved sigh as the door swung shut behind the shapely ass of his would-be nanny, his relief almost immediately replaced by annoyance at his right-hand man. What was Collins thinking? Weren't nannies supposed to be kindly gray-haired ladies, like Mrs. Doubtfire? Without the penis, naturally.

He slumped down at his desk and scrubbed a hand through his hair. As much as he wanted to blame his assistant, it was his fault, too. Collins might have screened the résumés the agency had sent over, but if Rhys had paid closer attention, taken time to have more than a five-minute phone conversation with the woman his assistant had picked as the best of the bunch, he would have realized she was all wrong for the position.

Beth had been gone three years, but sharing a house—even an eight-bedroom mansion with a large terrace, private pool, and four-car garage—with an attractive, single woman under the age of forty still felt disloyal to her. Especially since it was his fault she was dead.

He pushed away the guilt he'd fought like a demon every damn day for the last one thousand–plus days and pressed the intercom. Before he could speak, the door cracked open and Collins stuck his head in.

"It's customary to knock." Rhys released the button. No need for an intercom when the man you were looking for was standing right in front of you.

"It's also customary not to fire the new nanny before she starts," Collins shot back, entering the room fully and closing the door behind him.

"News travels fast. Book Miss Worthington on the first flight back to New York and line up some more experienced candidates for me to interview." Translation: kind, matronly women in their fifties or sixties who smell like fresh-baked cookies and read *Green Eggs and Ham* on demand. Rhys flipped open the file for his conference call in—he checked his Patek Philippe Nautilus—five minutes, hoping Collins would take the hint and consider the subject closed.

Instead of following his marching orders, Collins took a seat in one of the guest chairs. So much for taking the hint. "Can I speak freely?"

Rhys reached into his desk drawer and pulled out a Darth Vader PEZ dispenser. Unlike some collectors, he didn't believe in hiding his treasures on a shelf or behind glass, with the exception of a few especially valuable pieces. A robot PEZ dispenser from the 1950s. A pre-1989 Batman PEZ in its original packaging. And his prize possession, a rare Mickey Mouse soft head prototype worth over seven thousand dollars.

He pulled back Darth's head, and a yellow tablet popped out. Lemon. Beth's favorite. She'd laughed at his obsession with the iconic candy, but eventually she'd come to appreciate the kitschy containers. Hell, she'd bought a good portion of them for him, including the one he held in his hand. He ran a thumb over Darth's helmet as he stuck the tablet in his mouth and sucked on it. "If I said no, would that stop you?"

"Probably not." Collins smirked. It was a good thing he'd made himself virtually indispensable, or Rhys would have canned his ass, too.

He consulted his watch again. "You've got four minutes."

"You're making a mistake sending Miss Worthington away."

"You don't say?" Rhys leaned back in his chair and crossed an ankle over his knee. "What makes you think that?"

Collins hesitated, then shrugged. "Call it a gut feeling."

Rhys had a gut feeling, too, but it was telling him the more distance between him and Mallory Worthington, the better. He dropped another candy into his mouth and tossed the dispenser onto his desk. "Forgive me if I don't trust your gut."

"It's not like you to dismiss someone without good cause."

Rhys arched a brow. "Who says I don't have good cause?"

"You just met the woman," Collins said pointedly. "What could she have done in the minutes you spent with her to justify letting her go?"

Rhys stood and crossed to the rolling bar cart in the corner. He needed alcohol to get through this conversation. He poured himself two fingers of eighteen-year-old Macallan into a tumbler, added an extra splash for good measure, then turned back to his assistant.

He could have told Collins to fuck off. That he was the boss, and his reasons for sending Mallory Worthington packing were none of his assistant's goddamn business.

But shutting himself away from the rest of the world meant there weren't a lot of options when he needed a sounding board. In the seven years Collins had worked for him—especially in the three since Beth's death—he'd become more than an employee. He'd become a trusted confidant, the one person Rhys could rely on to tell him the whole ugly, unvarnished truth.

The one person Rhys could come close to calling a friend.

Rhys sat back down at his desk and sipped his scotch. "We both know why having her here isn't a good idea."

"You mean because she's young, attractive, and available, and so are you?"

Rhys wanted to wipe the persistent smirk off his assistant's face. "How do you know she's available?"

"She took this job and moved almost fifteen hundred miles from the city she called home at the drop of a hat." Collins leaned forward, resting his elbows on his knees. "I'd say she wasn't worried about leaving anyone behind."

"All the more reason why she can't stay." Rhys downed another gulp of scotch, relishing the burn as it streamed down his throat.

"Stop me if I'm overstepping my bounds…"

"Stop."

"…but it's been three years since the accident."

"Beth's death was no accident." Rhys slammed his glass down on the desk. Scotch sloshed over his hand and onto the blotter, splashing the PEZ dispenser. "It was murder."

And he was the one responsible.

"She wouldn't want you living this way," Collins persisted. "If you can call cutting yourself off from civilization living."

Damn stubborn man, made all the more annoying by the fact that deep down, Rhys knew he was right. Beth would hate what he'd become. Not that he was admitting it to Collins.

"Look around. This place is practically a palace, not a one-room shack in the middle of the woods. And I'm not cut off from civilization. That's what I've got you for."

Collins narrowed his eyes. "What about Oliver? Is this what she'd want for him?"

"She'd want him alive." Rhys tossed back the rest of his scotch, stood, and crossed to the bar cart for a refill. "I'm doing what I have to in order to keep him safe."

He might not have been able to protect Beth, but he wouldn't make the same mistake with his son. Even if it meant making him a virtual prisoner for the time being. Rhys didn't want to think about the inevitable changes as his son grew older. High school. College. He couldn't keep Oliver to himself forever.

But he could for now, and as long as possible.

Collins let out a long, loud sigh. "I understand your motivation, even if I don't necessarily agree with your methods."

"Does that mean the Spanish Inquisition is over?"

"No. But I'll grant you a temporary reprieve."

"I'll take it." Rhys poured another generous two fingers of scotch into his glass, swirled, sipped, and stared down his assistant. "Don't you have a plane reservation to make?"

Not one to back down, at least when they were mano a mano, Collins met his gaze. "You're still determined to send her away?"

Rhys continued to swirl, sip, and stare.

"All right." Collins stood a little more abruptly than necessary and straightened his tie. No matter how many times Rhys told him to lose the formal attire in the Florida heat, the man insisted on dressing like an undertaker when he was on duty, his only concession to the weather the deck shoes he wore on the launch. "Have it your way."

"I always do. That's the benefit of being the boss."

"Would you consider a small compromise?"

"How small?"

"Let her stay until we get a replacement. Mrs. Flannigan's got enough on her plate with the housekeeping, and she's not getting any younger. It's not fair for her to do double duty."

Rhys tipped his head back and looked skyward. Or more accurately, ceiling-ward. When Collins was right, he was right. The older woman had signed on to do light housework, laundry, and the occasional meal, not keep up with an overactive preschooler. It wasn't fair of him to put his hang-ups before her job satisfaction and his son's well-being. He brought his gaze back down and gave Collins the slightest, almost imperceptible nod. "Fine. But I want someone here by the end of the week. Two, tops."

Fourteen days, for the good of his housekeeper and his son. That didn't dishonor Beth's memory, did it?

"Done." Collins brushed his hands together triumphantly, as if to emphasize that the matter was settled, and he had, at least in part, emerged the victor. "And let the record show I still think you're making a mistake not giving Miss Worthington a chance."

"Duly noted." Rhys raised his glass in a mock salute.

With a salute of his own, Collins spun on his heel, crossed the room, and disappeared out the door, leaving Rhys the way he found him. The way he spent most of his days, with the exception of the all-too-rare moments he had with his son.

Alone.

• • •

"Here you are, Miss Worthington." Mrs. Flannigan led Mallory into a room more fit for a VIP than a nanny. "I hope you'll find it to your liking."

Mallory bit her lip to stop herself from asking the gray-haired housekeeper to call her by her first name. What did it matter? And what did it matter if Mallory approved of the accommodations or not? She wouldn't be staying long.

Her gut twisted at the thought, and she let out an

involuntary sob.

"Everything all right, dear?" Mrs. Flannigan asked, staring at Mallory expectantly. The woman must think she was a few fries short of a Happy Meal.

"Yes." Mallory gave the housekeeper a smile she hoped read reassuring and not psycho ax murderer waiting to strike. "Thank you."

"Collins brought up your bag." Mrs. Flannigan gestured to the corner, where her overnight tote sat on an overstuffed chair. "Ring if there's anything else you need. The intercom is on the wall next to the bed."

"Thanks, I will." Mallory spotted the boxes she'd sent at the foot of the enormous four-poster bed. No use unpacking. She'd slap new labels on them and call the shipping company to pick them up. Or maybe she could dig out her nail polishes. She had the sudden urge to repaint her toenails. Something to match her mood, like Here Today Aragon Tomorrow or Got Myself Into a Jam-balaya. She deserved a little pampering after uprooting her entire life and traveling hundreds of miles just to be summarily dismissed by a condescending, arrogant, self-righteous...

"Breakfast is at eight." Mrs. Flannigan's light, lilting voice interrupted Mallory's rapidly escalating internal tirade. There weren't enough adjectives in the English language for her to express her extreme dislike—she reserved the word "hate" for things like tabloid journalism and undercooked seafood and the cancer that stole her childhood and almost her life—of Rhys Dalton. She supposed she should be grateful he was feeding her before shipping her out.

"Thanks," she said again, forcing a smile so the kindly older woman wouldn't spot her inner turmoil. "What time will Collins be taking me to the airport?"

"Airport?" Mrs. Flannigan's brows drew together in confusion.

Great. Now Mallory had the added embarrassment of having to explain the whole humiliating situation. Out loud. To a virtual stranger. Making it seem that much more real and five times more mortifying. She cleared her throat. "I guess you haven't heard. I won't be staying."

Mrs. Flannigan clucked her tongue. "I don't know where you're getting your information, but my instructions were very clear. You'll be here at least a week, maybe more. Mr. Dalton wants you to meet Oliver in the morning and help out until the new nanny gets here."

Mallory went from confused to majorly pissed off in a nanosecond. Who did this guy think he was, ordering her to hang around and wait for her replacement to show up? As if she weren't humiliated enough already. She was a highly skilled, sought-after culinary artist, not some lackey content to do his bidding.

"Where is he?" She clenched and unclenched her fists at her sides. "I want to talk to him. Now."

"Do you think that's wise?"

No, she didn't. But for maybe the first time in her life she was going to stand up for herself. Wasn't that what this whole stunt—her father's word—was all about? Taking charge of her life, making her own decisions, not letting anyone else determine the course of her future? "Just take me to him. Please."

"Well." The older woman leaned in and whispered conspiratorially, even though there was no one else in hearing distance. "If I were you, I'd let him sleep on it. Tomorrow's a brand-new day. Play your cards right, and you might change his mind."

"And convince him to put me on the next plane home?"

"No." Mrs. Flannigan's silvery gray eyes twinkled. "And convince him to let you stay. Permanently. That's what you want, isn't it?"

Was it? When she left New York, Mallory was so sure she was doing the right thing. But now? Was this where she was supposed to be, or had she been in such a hurry to escape, to go somewhere —anywhere—she could start with a clean slate, one that didn't have "cancer survivor" written all over it, that she'd run to the wrong place?

She shook her head. "What I want doesn't matter. Mr. Dalton made it clear I'm not his idea of good nanny material."

"So show him you are." Mrs. Flannigan moved to the bed and started to turn down the sheets.

Show him you are. Could it be that simple?

"I'll leave you to think it over." The housekeeper finished off the bed with a pat and headed toward the door. "Things always look different in the light of day."

Mallory watched her leave, then scanned the pile of boxes for the one marked TOILETRIES. A new pedicure was definitely in order. But she had a different color in mind. Something along the lines of Tanacious Spirit or No Stopping Me Now. Because if she was going to change Rhys Dalton's mind about firing her, she'd need all the help she could get.

Chapter Three

There was nothing like an early-morning run on the beach as the sun turned the sky pink. The rumble and hiss of the surf underscoring the pounding of his sneakers on the wet sand, his only company the gulls and pipers foraging in the washed-up kelp. A chance to reflect on the day before. To plan the day ahead.

And, if Rhys was honest, to excise thoughts of a certain striking blonde who had invaded his home and his brain.

He pushed himself harder, trying to sweat her out of his system. It ran in rivulets down his face and neck, soaking his T-shirt. When he reached the rock jetty at the end of the beach, he pulled up short and bent over at the waist, his breath coming in quick, ragged gasps.

It had been a mistake bringing Mallory to Flamingo Key. But it was one he was in the process of fixing ASAP. Until then, he'd keep his distance. With more than twenty rooms and an entire island to work with, that shouldn't be a problem.

His resolve steeled, Rhys straightened, wiped his brow with the hem of his T-shirt, and started to retrace his steps, picking up the pace as he went. By the time he reached the stretch of beach in front of the house, he was winded and drenched with sweat again, the warm, peaceful waters of the Caribbean screaming for him to dive in and cool off.

It was a siren song he heard on almost every morning run but usually ignored, in too much of a rush to get a head start on his business day before the rest of the world woke up. But not today. Today he had a damn good reason to stay on the beach as long as humanly possible.

He kicked off his sneakers and peeled off his socks and shirt, leaving him in only lightweight running shorts. Not his typical swimming attire, but beggars couldn't be choosers.

As he neared the water's edge, he could make out a small silhouette cutting through the waves like an Olympic medalist. No way either of the Flannigans could swim like that. Or Oliver, who had just learned to put his head under water and preferred their infinity pool to the salty ocean. Collins was a strong swimmer and sometimes took a dip before breakfast, but he'd taken the launch to Key West for supplies.

Which left only one possible person. The very person Rhys was trying like hell to avoid.

The smartest course of action would be to get the fuck out of there before she saw him. But then she stood, rising from the water like a goddess, and slicked back her long blond hair. The movement arched her back and thrust her breasts against the thin, almost sheer fabric of her one-piece swimsuit. It left so little to the imagination it might as well have been a dental floss bikini.

Rhys froze, all his good intentions—and any semblance of rational thought—evaporated. He stood transfixed, wishing his damn running shorts were a little less form-fitting, as Mallory wrung out her hair and blinked the water from her eyes.

The second she spotted him, the relaxed smile playing around the corners of her lips disappeared, replaced by a hard, thin line. Her hands balled into fists then slowly loosened, as if she had to will her fingers to relax.

"Miss Worthington." He nodded a greeting. "Great minds think alike."

"I hope it's not a problem." She folded her arms across her chest, hiding her scantily clad breasts from view. He didn't know whether to say a silent prayer of thanks or curse his lousy luck. "Oliver's still sleeping, and Mrs. Flannigan said he wouldn't be out of bed for at least an hour."

"It's hard to resist the call of the Caribbean. You might as well take advantage of it while you're here."

A shadow crossed her beautiful face, and her eyes darted to the beach behind him. "Right. I'll let you get to your swim."

He mentally kicked himself in the ass.

Way to go, dickweed. Remind her she's got one foot out the door.

As guilty as he felt for disrespecting his wife's memory by sharing his house, even temporarily, with an attractive woman, Beth would have hated the way he was treating Mallory. He could almost hear her scolding him in that sweet, singsongy voice that betrayed her Southern roots, the voice that haunted his dreams, waking and sleeping.

She's come all this way to help you. To help our son. The least you can do is be polite.

Rhys rubbed a hand over his jaw, scratchy with early-morning stubble. "You don't have to leave on my account. The ocean's big enough for the two of us."

"I'm sure it is, but I was about to head back to the house." Mallory gave her hair another twist, wringing out a few more drops of water that fell to her chest and clung there, defying gravity as they shimmered in the yellow-gold of the rising sun. "I want to be showered and dressed before Oliver wakes up."

The mere mention of the word "shower" had Rhys's sex-starved brain spinning off in a thousand directions. Her swimsuit didn't leave much to the imagination, but his mind was more than willing and totally able to fill in the blanks. Slick, soapy skin. Water running over her soft curves and down her milky thighs. Her head tipped back, eyes closed, a low moan escaping her parted lips as she lathered up her hair.

"Mr. Dalton? What about breakfast?"

Her clipped words jerked him back to the present. "I'm sorry. Did you say something?"

She rolled her doe eyes. "I asked if Oliver had a favorite breakfast. I know I won't be here long, but I thought I'd start off on the right foot by making something he likes."

"Pancakes, I think. Or waffles." Or was it French toast? Scrambled eggs? Rhys swore under his breath. Was he so preoccupied with work he didn't know his own son's food preferences?

"That's okay. I'll ask Mrs. Flannigan."

Her words said okay, but there was no missing the judgment in her tone. It washed over him like a rogue wave, making him feel like even more of a shit than he already did.

Before he could come up with some sort of response, something to redeem himself—although he had no fucking clue why he gave a damn about the opinion of a woman he barely knew and didn't plan on getting to know—she was on the move, the waves lapping at her knees, then her ankles as she headed for shore. His eyes tracked her as she walked away, the subtle sway of her hips making things stir south of the border.

When she was out of sight, he turned and dived headfirst into the rippling water. He surfaced and swam parallel to the shore, pounding through the waves with confident, powerful strokes. He wasn't sure what he hoped it would accomplish more, cooling down his overactive sex drive or washing away his sins.

Unfortunately, it did neither.

Failing to protect Beth. Choosing his work over their son. Lusting after Mallory. A little swim in the surf, no matter how punishing, wasn't going to erase all that.

Not that it stopped him from trying.

• • •

"What's that?" A four-year-old nose wrinkled and eyes the same warm chestnut as their owner's father's narrowed at the plate Mallory placed on the eat-in counter.

"French toast." She turned briefly to the stove to flip another slice of thickly battered brioche bread before swiveling back to face the little boy who was her responsibility until further notice. "Mrs. Flannigan says it's your favorite."

Oliver wrinkled his nose again and pushed the plate away. "That's not French toast. French toast isn't fat. And it doesn't have strawberries on it. I hate strawberries."

What kid doesn't like strawberries?

Oliver crossed his scrawny arms over his bony chest, hiding the Captain America logo on his pajamas, and glared at her with an intensity that rivaled his father's.

This kid, apparently. Maybe she shouldn't have been so quick to send Mrs. Flannigan away.

No, she had this. The poor woman had enough to do without having to watch over them like a mother hen. And Mallory had dealt with more than her fair share of tough customers at the Worthington. Handling a picky preschooler couldn't be that different. Could it?

She inched the plate back toward him. "It's brioche bread. That's why it's so thick. And I can take the strawberries off. Or give you another slice."

Oliver shook his head, his glare not losing one bit of its

ferocity. She'd only met him a few minutes ago, but she could already tell he was Rhys Dalton's mini-me, from the eyes to the attitude. "I hate bee-yotch bread."

Mallory swallowed a laugh and fought hard to keep the corners of her mouth from curling. "Brioche. And how do you know you hate it if you haven't tried it?"

He cocked his head. "How do you know I haven't tried it?"

Damn. The kid had her there. Pretty solid logic for a four-year-old. Another trait no doubt passed down from his no-nonsense father.

This called for a little negotiation.

She turned back to the stove, flicked the now perfectly toasted brioche from the pan onto a plate, and swapped it with the one on the counter before shutting off the burner. "Tell you what. Try one piece. Just one. And if you don't like it, I'll make you thin French toast, like you're used to."

It would kill her to use the glue-flavored, mass-produced crap most people thought of as bread, but if the way to Oliver's heart was through his stomach, she'd swallow her master-chef pride and make the kid what he wanted.

He rested his elbows on the counter and put his chin in his hands. "How big of a piece?"

She held up two fingers about an inch apart. "This big."

He frowned and held up two fingers of his own with half an inch between them. "This big. With syrup. The real kind, in the glass bottle Mrs. Flannigan brought back from New Hamster."

Mallory found herself battling back another grin. "I think you mean New Hampshire."

"She and Mr. Flannigan went there on their second honeymoon to look at the leaves. And you have to heat it up in the microwave like she does."

Kid drove a hard bargain. She stuck out a hand for him

to shake. "Deal."

He took it, his small hand disappearing in hers but his grip surprisingly strong. "Deal."

She found a bottle shaped like a maple leaf in the refrigerator, poured some into a ceramic creamer, and put it in the microwave, setting the timer for thirty seconds. When it dinged, she took out the creamer and slid it across the counter to Oliver.

His eyes widened. "Aren't you going to pour it for me? Mrs. Flannigan always does."

"I don't know." She tapped a finger against her cheek, pretending to study him with the absorption of Michelangelo painting the ceiling of the Sistine Chapel. "You look like a big boy to me. I'll bet you can do it all by yourself."

He sat up straighter on his stool, puffing out his puny preschooler chest. "I am a big boy."

"I thought so." She leaned in and lowered her voice to a clandestine whisper. "How much do you use? A little or a lot?"

"A lot." His fingers curled around the handle of the creamer.

"Me, too," she agreed, still whispering as if their shared love of syrup was a state secret. "I like my French toast swimming in the stuff."

"Yeah. Swimming." He giggled and tipped the creamer over his plate until it was almost empty.

"Here." She held out a fork and a butter knife. "I'll bet you can cut it all by yourself, too."

He pursed his lips and pushed her hand away. "Mrs. Flannigan says I make too much of a mess."

"So we'll clean it up." She extended the fork and knife to him again. "There's sponges and disinfectant for the counter. We can throw your pajamas in the wash. Problem solved. Unless..." She let her voice trail off.

His brow furrowed. "Unless what?"

"You don't melt if you get wet, do you?"

"You mean like the Wicked Witch of the West?"

She nodded. "Exactly."

"No way." He shook his head so hard his platinum curls—the color inherited from his mother, she assumed—flew around his face. "I like the water. I'm a real good swimmer. I can even dunk my head. My daddy teached me."

"Oh, he did, did he?" From the way his daddy acted yesterday, she was surprised he remembered he had a son, never mind taught him how to swim. But first impressions could be misleading. She knew that better than anyone.

Not that her opinion of her boss—good or bad—mattered one iota if she couldn't convince him to let her stay.

"Yep." Oliver's response jerked her back to the present. "He says I'm a fish."

"Then you'll be easy to clean up, too." She handed over the utensils. "Have at it."

He gripped the fork and knife in his pudgy fingers and started to saw away, predictably splattering syrup over everything in a three-foot radius. After a few minutes, he succeeded in separating a small square of toast and spearing it with his fork. He stared at it for what seemed like hours before lifting it to his mouth and nibbling at one corner.

Mallory pulled up a stool outside the danger zone and reached for the plate Oliver had rejected. "What do you think?"

He nibbled again.

Licked his lips.

Nibbled.

Licked.

"Not as good as Mrs. Flannigan's," he finally announced, popping the rest of the square into his mouth and continuing through a mouthful of food. "But it's okay, I guess."

"Thanks, I guess." High praise coming from a kid used to having the best of everything. Except French toast, obviously. Mallory mentally patted herself on the back and started in on her own plate.

"Can we go to the beach?" Oliver asked, reattacking his food with his knife and fork.

"When you finish your breakfast."

Mallory's head snapped up at the gravelly, already-too-familiar voice of her employer, lounging against the archway between the kitchen and living room as if he owned the world. Which he probably could if he wanted to.

He'd showered and changed, but if she thought being fully dressed would make him less distracting she was way off base. She'd had a glimpse of what was underneath his short-sleeved polo and neatly pressed khakis, and that was something she wasn't going to unsee any time soon. Not that she wanted to.

"Would you like some French toast?" she asked, staring at a button in the middle of his chest. Seemed as safe a place to look as any other. "I can whip up another batch."

He didn't say anything for a long, torturous moment, the awkward silence forcing her gaze up the strong column of his tanned throat and past his freshly shaven, chiseled jaw until her eyes locked with his. The cool appraisal in their chocolate depths shook her to the core, and she sucked in a quick breath.

What was wrong with her? He was just a guy. Okay, an extraordinarily good-looking guy. Like eleven-on-a-scale-of-one-to-ten good-looking. But she'd spent her life surrounded by "the beautiful people," as her sister called them. Why did this guy have to be the one who made her girlie parts wake up and do the Macarena?

"He never eats breakfast," Oliver piped up, his youthful high-pitched voice cutting through the sexual tension that had descended on the room like a thick fog. At least, she thought it was sexual tension. Maybe it was completely one-sided, and Rhys Dalton was mentally counting the days until he could get rid of her. "Right, Dad?"

"Just coffee for me," Rhys finally answered, his eyes never leaving hers. "Black."

She broke his gaze and stood, losing the battle of wills but determined to win the war. Her appetite gone, she took her plate to the sink and scraped the remains of her French toast into the disposal. "You know breakfast is the most important meal of the day, right?"

"That's what Grover says on *Sesame Street*," Oliver added in between bites, his plate almost empty. "He can't be Super Grover until he eats his breakfast."

Mallory shot him a thumbs-up for having her back.

"I'll take it under advisement. But for now, coffee will do. I have a Skype session with one of our design engineers in fifteen minutes and a lot of material to go over before then."

Rhys ruffled his son's hair as he crossed past him on the way to the rack of K-Cups on the counter next to the Keurig machine, and her insides did a funny little flip. Something about the small, affectionate gesture gave her all the feels. It was hard to reconcile with his aloofness the night before, and for the second time that morning, she questioned her rush to judgment.

The man was a hot mess of maddening contradictions. Working for him would be one heck of a challenge. But it was one she desperately wanted the chance to conquer, if for no other reason than to prove to herself she could succeed on her own, outside the sphere of her parents' influence, without any special treatment because of a disease she'd had—and beaten—years ago.

She opened the cabinet next to the sink and reached for a mug. "Don't say I didn't warn you when ten o'clock rolls around and you can't focus on anything but your stomach grumbling."

"My stomach doesn't grumble. And I never lose focus."

He went to take the cup from her, and their fingers brushed. The brief contact was like touching a live wire, making her jerk back and sending the mug clattering to the floor, where it shattered on the hard tiles.

"I'm sorry." She bent and started picking up the shards. "I'm not always such a klutz."

"I'll help." Oliver hopped down from his stool, his bare feet slapping the terra-cotta.

"No," Rhys snapped, holding up a hand and freezing his son in his tracks. "I've got this. You two go upstairs and get ready for the beach."

"Are you sure?" Mallory surveyed the damage. Ceramic slivers all over the floor. Counter covered in syrup. Dirty dishes in the sink. Her fault, and her responsibility to fix.

"Please," Rhys hissed, inclining his head toward Oliver. "Before he hurts himself."

"Right." Some nanny she was turning out to be, putting her feelings before Oliver's safety.

"Come on." The little boy stuck out a sticky hand to her. "I want to build a sandcastle and catch hermit crabs and go swimming in the pool. Then you can make me grilled cheese for lunch. On bee-yotch bread. Okay?"

"Okay." She stepped gingerly across the kitchen, tossed the remnants she'd collected into the trash, and took Oliver's grubby hand. The morning hadn't been a complete disaster. She'd gained his trust. And turned him on to brioche bread.

She only hoped the father was as easy to win over as the son.

Chapter Four

Rhys scrawled his signature across the bottom of yet another document and pushed it across his desk. Paperwork was one of his least favorite duties as chairman and CEO of Argos Research and Development, the tech company he'd started from his dorm room at Stanford. He'd much rather be brainstorming ways to expand into new markets or working on the company's latest gadget to improve lives, like the robotic arm that propelled Argos into the Fortune 500. But as much as he loved the creative side of things, the administrative crap was a necessary evil. "Is that the last of them?"

"One more." Collins took the signed document and replaced it with another, thicker one. "The employment contract for the new CFO. Legal approved it yesterday. I've tabbed where you need to sign."

"It's about time." Rhys leafed through the document, reading as he signed where Collins had indicated. "I gave the board the go-ahead to hire him weeks ago."

"Legal had to do some negotiating. His attorney had some issues with the wording of the noncompete clause."

Rhys flipped to that section of the contract. "I take it Legal is satisfied with the revisions?"

"Yes. Baker felt comfortable reducing the term from a year to six months as long as the nondisclosure agreement was in place. He says to call him if you want to pick his brain."

"I trust his judgment." Mark Baker had been the head of the company's in-house legal team since it had gone public. He'd proved his worth time and time again, and Rhys didn't make it a habit of second-guessing valued employees.

"Nice to know you respect someone's opinion other than your own," Collins muttered.

Rhys lifted an eyebrow. "Excuse me?"

The sounds of Mallory's voice and his son's laughter followed by splashing drifted through the open window—the house had central air-conditioning, but nothing beat a cool late-afternoon breeze—and Rhys had a sudden sinking suspicion of what was coming next.

"Are you still planning on firing Miss Worthington?"

Rhys signed the last page of the contract with a flourish, closed the document, and practically threw it across the desk at Collins. "I wouldn't exactly call it firing."

"What would you call it then?"

Good question. If he'd been paying more attention, he never would have hired Mallory in the first place. He was only trying to put things back the way they were. Or the way they would have been if he hadn't screwed up. Was there a word for that?

"Oliver seems to like her," Collins continued, not waiting for Rhys to come up with an answer. "I haven't seen him this happy since…"

He ran a finger under his collar before finishing his sentence. "In a long time."

Rhys shifted in his seat. As much as he didn't want to admit it, Collins had a point. It had only been a few days since her arrival, and already Oliver and Mallory were almost inseparable. But that didn't mean his son couldn't form as strong a bond with someone else.

Did it?

He steepled his fingers under his chin and bent forward. "Shouldn't you be screening new nannies? I haven't seen one candidate."

"I guess that answers my question." Collins gathered up the papers Rhys signed and stuffed them into a folder. "And technically, Mallory's not a nanny. She's a personal chef who has a lot of experience with children."

Rhys picked up a pen and tapped it against his desk blotter. "It's Mallory now, is it?"

"I'll have a list for you tomorrow morning," Collins said, ignoring the barb. "With résumés. And photos. But for the record…"

"I know, I know." Rhys traded the pen for one of his ever-present PEZ dispensers—Kermit the Frog this time—then leaned back and propped his feet up on the desk, absently flicking Kermit's head. Open. Closed. Open. Closed. The rhythm was soothing, almost Zen. To him, at least. From experience, he knew it annoyed the shit out of Collins. Which, given their current conversation, he considered an added bonus. "You think I'm making a mistake."

Trouble was, part of Rhys was starting to think so, too.

"Got it in one." Collins tucked the folder under his arm and stood. "Is there anything else you need before I clock out? It's my bowling night on the mainland."

"You can go." Rhys popped a purple PEZ in his mouth. It had its usual calming effect, same as it had since childhood. PEZ and physics, two things he could always count on. "Just be sure I have those résumés and pictures first thing tomorrow."

"If you insist."

"I do." He had to. For his own sanity.

He spent another half hour in the wake of Collins's departure trying to answer emails and check on the progress of Argos's newest venture. Trying, but not succeeding thanks to the continued laughter and splashing from the pool, only feet from his open window.

Was he making the right decision sending her away? Beth would want their son to be happy. And Collins was right. Mallory certainly seemed to make Oliver happy. But that didn't change the fact that it felt wrong living with a woman he was attracted to. And as much as he wanted to, he couldn't deny the pull she had on him.

The question was, could he fight it for his son's sake?

He pushed his chair away from his desk and stood. His productivity was shot to shit. Time to blow off some steam. Maybe lift some weights in his home gym or…

A shrill, childlike scream he immediately recognized as his son's changed his path. Within seconds, he was poolside where Mallory sat on one of the cushioned lounge chairs with Oliver in her lap, examining his foot.

"What happened?" he barked, the words coming out more harshly than he intended. He took a steadying breath and made a conscious effort to soften his tone. "Is he hurt?"

"Bee sting," she explained, not looking up from the wound. "It's a little red and swollen. Has he been stung before?"

"No." Rhys gave his head a slight shake. There was that time in Central Park. The three of them had gone to the zoo. Beth brought a picnic lunch, and they spread out a blanket on the Great Lawn. Their meal had been cut short when Oliver got some sort of bugbite, but Rhys was pretty sure a spider was the culprit. "I don't think so."

"Which is it?" Mallory raised her head to look at him, and the disapproval in her eyes made him wish she hadn't.

"No," he said with a bit more confidence. "He hasn't."

"It hurts," Oliver wailed, tears streaking down his tanned face. "I hate bees. Bees suck."

"Don't say suck." Mallory smoothed a damp blond curl off his cheek. "And you don't hate bees. Without bees, we wouldn't have flowers."

Oliver stuck out his chin. "I hate flowers, too."

"No." She chuckled and pressed a kiss to the top of his son's head. "You don't."

Rhys took a step toward them, then stopped. It was almost painful watching them. Like they were in their own world, an insulated bubble where only the two of them existed. He was a mere observer. No, worse. An interloper. His stomach clenched at the realization.

"You'll be fine, I promise." Mallory laid Oliver on the chaise next to her and stood, oblivious to Rhys's inner torment. "Your dad can take care of you while I go inside and find something to make the pain go away."

Any sliver of relief Rhys felt at her suggestion was immediately snuffed out by his son's response.

"No." Oliver bolted upright and grabbed her forearm, his little-boy fingers barely reaching around her slim wrist. The desperation in his voice reminded Rhys of his own when the NYPD had shown up at his office that Norman Rockwell–perfect fall day three years ago, changing his life and his son's forever. "Don't leave me. Make him go."

With his free hand, Oliver stabbed a stubby finger at Rhys.

"You don't mean that." Mallory at least had the decency to blush.

"It's okay." If having your heart ripped out by your four-year-old progeny was okay. But his son's well-being was more important than his injured ego. "What do you need?"

Mallory hesitated as if she was going to argue with him,

then glanced from Oliver's tearstained face to the white-knuckled hand still clutching her wrist and apparently thought the better of it. "He might have a mild allergy. Do you have any baking soda to neutralize the venom? Apple cider vinegar works, too."

"In the kitchen." He hoped. He might have to ransack the place to find them. The only thing he ever touched in there was the Keurig. Mrs. Flannigan had it memorized down to the last tablespoon, but he'd given her and her husband the night off, so they could hitch a ride on the launch with Collins and catch a movie in Key West. "I'll be right back."

He spun on his heel and in two loping strides was at the sliding glass doors separating the pool area from the house when a plaintive wail stopped him.

"Daddy."

He turned and met the wide, watery eyes of his son. Mallory sat next to Oliver on the chaise, stroking his back the same way Beth used to do when he was cranky or tired or injured, like a knife to Rhys's already-shredded heart.

"Hurry. Please. It hurts real bad."

Rhys resisted the urge to gather him up in his arms. Mallory had the sympathy thing covered. What Oliver needed from him was strength. "I know it does. You're very brave."

Oliver puffed out his chest and let out something that sounded like a cross between a hiccup and a sob. "That's right. I am. Like you."

Now it was Rhys's chest that swelled. His relationship with Oliver had been strained since Beth's death. It wasn't that he didn't love his son. More like he loved him too much, so damn much he'd unconsciously—or consciously—shut down, afraid of losing someone else close to him. Like keeping his son at arm's length emotionally would lessen the pain.

Idiot.

But maybe it wasn't a lost cause. Oliver was young. There was time for Rhys to change course.

He swallowed the lump in his throat. "I'll be back as fast as I can. Until then, take care of Miss Worthington."

Oliver's forehead wrinkled. "Who's Miss Worthington?"

"He means me," Mallory explained, grinning.

"I'll take care of you," Oliver said with all the seriousness of a priest hearing confession. "I'm a good taker-carer."

Rhys shared a smile with his son before disappearing into the house. It might not be much, but it was a start. One he wanted to build on.

If he only knew how.

• • •

"How goes it, Fräulein Maria? Has the handsome head of the household fallen victim to your charms yet?"

Mallory freed her hair from its utilitarian, kid-friendly ponytail, shook it out, and sank down onto her eyelet comforter. After the beesting drama of that afternoon, all she wanted was a warm shower, a cold drink, and a good book. Instead, she'd made the mistake of dialing her sister, thinking four missed calls from Brooke meant some sort of emergency back in New York.

Sucker. She should have realized it was a fishing expedition. The only question was whether Brooke was casting for information on her own or whether their mother had put her up to it.

Either way, Mallory didn't have much to spill where her short-term boss was concerned. "Fräulein Maria?"

"You know, from *The Sound of Music.* Like her, you traveled to parts unknown to care for a widower and his motherless offspring."

"Except I'm not a nun, I can't sing, and Rhys Dalton has

one child, not seven."

Mallory could picture her sister waving a dismissive hand. "Unimportant details."

"How was Seattle?" she asked, crossing her fingers that Brooke would bite at the obvious attempt to change the subject. "Was Eli surprised when you showed up at his hotel?"

Her sister let out a long, melodramatic sigh, no doubt thinking of her husband, who'd been out west scouting opportunities for his real estate development firm. Mallory fought back her inner green monster. She was happy for her sister. Really, she was. But that didn't mean she couldn't also be a tad bit jealous Brooke had found her Prince Charming while Mallory was stuck kissing frogs.

Case in point: her last boyfriend. Sure, Hunter had looked great on paper. A doctor. From a good family. Knew all the right people, took her to all the right places. And Lord knows her parents adored him. But on paper was one thing. In person was another.

"Seattle was gray," Brooke answered. "And wet. And Eli was suitably shocked. Now I want to hear about you and Captain von Dreamy."

"I'm not Julie Andrews. And trust me, Rhys Dalton might be hot enough to bake cookies on, but he's no Christopher Plummer." Even the captain had let Maria stick around longer than a couple of weeks.

"Aha." Brooke's finger snap carried clearly across the phone line. "I was right. He is hot."

Crap. Good thing Mallory stayed on the right side of the law. She'd fold faster than a lawn chair if the cops ever interrogated her. "The point isn't that he's hot. The point is he's not falling for me, he's firing me."

"He's what?" Brooke's indignation was palpable, even over a thousand miles away.

Maybe Mallory shouldn't have said anything to her sister,

but she needed to unload on someone. She hadn't counted on how lonely she'd be so far from her only sibling.

She shook off the momentary melancholy and toed off her sandals, wiggling her freshly painted toes. She'd wound up going with a melon-peach with subtle pink undertones called You Got Nata On Me. A shot of adrenaline for her shaky self-confidence. Maybe later she'd do her fingernails to match for an extra boost, something she almost never did working in a commercial kitchen.

"I'm history as soon as he hires someone to take my place."

Or I convince him otherwise. That afternoon she'd felt her first flicker of hope. He'd have to be blind not to see how much Oliver was growing to care for her.

And the feeling was mutual. Not even a week, and already the little boy had wormed his way into her heart. He was funny and sweet and as lonely as she was. Two lost souls, swimming in a fishbowl.

She hated to admit it, but the father had started to grow on her, too. She'd seen glimpses of his softer side with Oliver. The tiny displays of affection. How he rushed to his son when he heard him scream after being stung by the bee. If only he let her stay long enough to…

"He can't do that," Brooke fumed, snapping Mallory out of her inspired reverie. She imagined her sister pacing the living room of her Brooklyn loft. "He can't fire you. I'll…"

"Yes, he can, and no, whatever crazy scheme you're dreaming up, you won't." Mallory glanced longingly at the bottle of chardonnay on the nightstand, begging for her to pop the cork. "It's called at-will employment. He can fire me for any reason he wants, or no reason at all."

At least that was what the agency told her when she called them with the news. Mallory was afraid they'd dump her as fast as Rhys Dalton, but according to Alison, her placement counselor, getting fired on first sight was more common than you'd think.

"Well, I'm sure the staffing agency will find you another job in no time." Brooke's confidence was almost contagious. "And you can stay with me and Eli until they ship you off again to who knows where. We've got two extra bedrooms. Take your pick."

Mallory chuckled and fell back onto the bed, her head cushioned by the hypoallergenic goose down pillows, covered in 500-thread-count Egyptian cotton. Okay, so she'd checked the tags. Sue her. They felt so darn good, she had to see what she was sleeping on. "What are you, a mind reader or something?"

"Just someone who understands needing a little—or a lot—of space from Mom and Dad."

Amen to that. Mallory had never understood her sister's rebellious streak before. She liked things to be predictable. Safe. Well-ordered. Pretty typical of cancer survivors, she'd learned thanks to myriad self-help books and weekly sessions with her therapist. They tended to fall into two camps: risk-averse and adventurous. The first did everything they could to stay healthy; the second viewed each day post-cancer as a gift, determined to live life to its fullest.

"You still there?" Brooke asked.

"Yeah." Mallory huffed a strand of hair out of her eyes and sighed. She really, really needed that wine. Stat. "Sorry. Got lost there for a minute. I was…"

Three sharp raps on the door had whatever excuse she'd been about to spout stuck in her throat. "Ma—Miss Worthington? Can I speak to you?"

Mallory froze.

"Ohmigod," she whispered into the phone. "It's him."

"Who, him?"

"Captain von Dreamy."

"You sound surprised." A wrapper crinkled, and Mallory pictured her sister opening a package of Ho Hos. Or a Slim Jim. No telling with Brooke's addiction to all things junk food. "He's your boss until further notice. Don't you talk?"

"No. Not usually." *Unless he thinks his son is in mortal peril.* "I mostly deal with Mrs. Flannigan, the housekeeper, or Collins, the..."

What was Collins exactly, anyway?

"Collins," she finished lamely.

"What's his deal?" Brooke asked through a mouthful of her chosen snack. "Von Dreamy, I mean."

"I don't know. It's like he goes out of his way to avoid me. On the rare occasions when he's forced to speak to me, he won't even use my first name."

"What does he call you?"

"Miss Worthington."

"Kinky."

Three more raps. "Miss Worthington?"

A tremor ran through her body. Why had she never noticed how her name sounded on his lips? Simultaneously formal and dirty, conjuring images of sweat-slicked bodies, satin sheets, and sleepless nights.

Damn her sister and her warped mind.

"Be right there," she called, moving the phone away from her mouth. "Just, uh, finishing something up."

Rhys shuffled his feet on the other side of the door. "I'm sorry to disturb you, but we need to talk."

"Hang up and answer the damn door," Brooke hissed. "But call me back the second he's gone. I want deets. And remember, if you get nervous, think WWJD."

Mallory frowned. "What would Jesus do?"

"No." If a smug smile had a sound, Brooke's voice, dripping over the airwaves like hot fudge on an ice cream sundae, was it. "What would Julie do?"

The line went dead. Mallory tossed her cell onto the bed beside her and sat up, stashing the sadly untouched bottle of chardonnay on the floor behind the nightstand. She didn't see any harm in having a glass of wine after hours. But there was no use poking the bear, even if he was about to give her walking papers.

"I'm coming." She winced at the unintended double meaning. She had sex on the brain, courtesy of her big sister. "I mean, I'll be right there."

She swung her legs over the side of the bed and stood, smoothing down her peasant blouse and khaki shorts. A quick glance in the full-length mirror on the back of her bathroom door told her she might as well not have bothered. She was a wrinkled, rumpled mess. And her hair—gah! She looked like she'd wrestled an alligator, gotten caught in a windstorm, and run a marathon, not necessarily in that order.

Presentable was out of the question. The best she could hope for was somewhere between mildly embarrassing and totally humiliating.

Not exactly how she wanted to face off with her hotter-than-the-sun employer, who most likely was about to inform her that her replacement was en route and her services were no longer necessary. But since she didn't have much—strike that, any—choice in the matter, she pulled on her metaphorical big-girl panties, adopted what she hoped was a neutral expression, and crossed to the door.

Like a condemned man walking to the gallows.

Chapter Five

What the hell was taking her so damn long?

Rhys resisted the urge to bang on the door again, crossing his arms and leaning against the frame to lessen the temptation. Every second that ticked by on his Patek Philippe further convinced him coming to Mallory like this, with his ego in shreds—and his head up his ass—was a mistake of epic proportions.

He wasn't a guy who was used to groveling. He was a mover. A shaker. A dealmaker. A hard-nosed negotiator who inspired awe—and a healthy dose of fear—in the hearts of all those lucky—or unlucky—enough to do business with him.

In short, he was the grovel-ee, not the fucking groveler. And there was only one force on earth strong enough to reverse that.

His love for his son.

He took a deep breath and steeled himself to knock a third time. Before his knuckles could strike the door, it swung open and Mallory stood before him, her hair free from its usual ponytail, falling in soft, wild waves around her face and shoulders.

Predictably, his thoughts drifted into X-rated territory. Not an uncommon occurrence since their encounter on the beach. Mallory, wet, breathless, and nearly naked, had become the star of his late-night erotic fantasies. And a few dirty daydreams, too.

Rhys did his best to ignore his reaction to her—something he had a feeling he'd be doing a whole hell of a lot if their conversation went as planned—and stuffed his hands into the pockets of his shorts. "I hope I'm not interrupting anything."

"No, not really." Mallory's cheeks flushed an appealing shade of pink. There was something irresistible about a woman who embarrassed so easily. It made him wonder if she blushed all over. "I was on the phone with my sister."

Way to win her over. Cut her off from her family. He took a step back and held his hands up, palms out. "I'm sorry. If you want to call her back, we can do this later."

"Do what?"

She blinked up at him, all wide-eyed innocence, and his hyperactive imagination went into overdrive, picturing all the things he'd like to do to her. Places he'd like to touch her, taste her…

"Mr. Dalton? Are you all right?"

Fuck no, he wasn't all right. He was all wrong. This was all wrong.

He had to stop thinking with his dick and remember why he was there. His son. "I wanted to talk to you about Oliver."

"Is something wrong?" The color drained from Mallory's face, and the hand still holding the doorknob tightened its grip. "He was fine when I put him to bed."

"Fast asleep. I just checked on him."

"Thank goodness." Some of the pink returned to Mallory's cheeks. "You scared me for a second."

"I'm sorry." Her obvious concern for his son made his

chest tighten and gave him the courage to forge ahead, doubts—and desires—be damned. "Can I come in?"

She opened the door wider and waved him inside. He was surprised to find in her short time there she'd managed to put her own personal stamp on the room. A scented candle burning on the nightstand. E-reader on the desk. Framed photos on the dresser.

"Sit down." She gestured to the bed.

On the sheets where she slept wearing what he imagined was damn near next to nothing, the Egyptian cotton caressing her bare flesh as she shifted in slumber?

No. Fucking. Way.

He wasn't a damn masochist. He opted for the desk chair instead. Hard and unforgiving and not in the least bit likely to stir up sexual fantasies.

"Whatever you want to talk about, it must be important for you to make a personal appearance," she continued, taking the spot she'd indicated for him. "Or was Collins busy?"

Rhys wanted to protest, but she had a point. Yes, he'd been avoiding her. And yes, he'd considered sending his assistant in his place. But some things a man had to do for himself.

Like admitting he'd royally screwed up.

"I want you to stay," he began, opting for the direct approach.

"Really?" She crossed one smooth, tanned leg over the other and leaned back on her palms. "Why the change of heart?"

"Oliver seems to like you."

And so do I. The words popped into his head uninvited, but once there they took hold. He did like her. Okay, so he'd barely taken the time to get to know her. But what he knew, he liked. And not just her body. He liked her ready smile. Her easygoing, playful nature with Oliver. The care and attention she lavished on everyone and everything from his son to the meals she prepared to the rest of the household staff.

Which was going to make staying the hell away from her that much harder.

Mallory swung one leg absently, unaware of battle raging inside him. "He's a great kid. I'm sure he'll get along fine with whoever you hire to replace me."

"He's had a hard time bonding with people since…" Rhys paused, never sure what to call the senseless act that robbed him of his wife and Oliver of a mother. He settled on the most benign word he could think of, not wanting to stir up any more sympathy than absolutely necessary. A useless emotion, if you asked him. No amount of tired platitudes and half-hearted condolences were going to bring Beth back. "Since the accident."

And…there it was. Sympathy in spades. Mallory's face morphed from polite interest to abject pity, complete with puppy-dog eyes and downturned lips. Rhys shifted in his seat and braced himself for the inevitable clichés.

I know what you're going through.

Time heals all wounds.

She's in a better place.

That last one always made him want to punch a wall. What did it even mean? What better place was there for a young mother than with her husband and son?

The puppy-dog eyes met his. "I'm sorry about your wife."

Huh. Interesting. None of the usual bullshit. Still, the last thing he wanted to talk about with this unfortunately attractive, unavoidably single female in the intimacy of her bedroom was Beth. What they'd had together. What they'd lost. He was there for one reason and one reason only. Once that mission was accomplished, he was hauling ass to safer ground as fast as his Top-Siders would take him.

He cleared his throat and pressed on. "Yes, well, Oliver's had a tough time connecting with women. We've gone through three nannies in the past six months. But he took to you right away."

She shrugged. "I think we're kindred spirits."

"How so?" Rhys crossed an ankle over his knee.

"It sounds trite, but I really do know how he feels. I've lost people close to me. And I've worked with kids who dealt with death every day."

He frowned, confused. Dealing with death every day? Who was this woman? "Your résumé says you're an executive chef."

"Is that why you fired me?" she shot back, uncrossing her legs and sitting straighter. "Because you didn't think I had enough experience with children?"

"Partly," he lied.

She was fully upright now, sitting ramrod straight and wagging a finger at him like some sexy schoolteacher. "I'm fully capable of handling a four-year-old. And you get the added benefit of my culinary skills. How many nannies can whip up a nutritious, kid-friendly, five-star meal without breaking a sweat?"

"You don't have to convince me of the error of my ways." This groveling thing was definitely not in his wheelhouse. He crossed his fingers he wasn't fucking it up too badly. "I asked you to stay."

"You did." Mallory's posture relaxed, and her expression softened. "I'm sorry. I guess I'm used to being on the defensive."

He wondered briefly what a striking, smart, seemingly sane woman would need to defend herself against but brushed it aside and focused on his immediate goal. "Does that mean you'll stay?"

She tilted her head and studied him thoughtfully. "On

two conditions."

"This should be interesting." He leaned forward, elbows on his knees.

"First." She held up a finger. "You have to have dinner with Oliver at least three—no, four times a week."

"Dinner?" Not quite what he'd expected. He thought she'd be angling for a raise. Extra days off. Matching contributions to her 401(k).

"Yes, you know. The meal that comes after lunch and before breakfast."

"I'm familiar with the concept."

"Are you familiar with the studies that show families who eat together feel less stressed, and children are more likely to try new foods, eat more fruits and vegetables, and have better grades?"

"Yes." At least, he dimly recalled reading something to that effect in one of the huge stacks of parenting books he and Beth had pored over in the joyous but nerve-racking months leading up to Oliver's birth. The memory made his eyes sting and his throat constrict.

He scrubbed a hand across his face to hide the tidal wave of conflicting emotions that always consumed him when thoughts of his wife surfaced. "But Oliver has to have dinner before six in order to be bathed and in bed by eight. My schedule makes it difficult for me wrap things up that early on a regular basis."

"Fine." She waved a hand dismissively, as if his concern were nothing more than a fly she could easily brush away. "You pick the meals. Any four."

"Breakfast included?" He was an early riser, and so was his son. He should be able to make that work.

She nodded. "Breakfast included."

"You drive a hard bargain, Miss Worthington." He tented his fingers. "What's number two?"

She crossed her legs, one flip-flop dangling from her brightly painted toes. What was that, the third or fourth color since she'd arrived? How often did she paint them? And why was he paying so much attention to her damn toenails?

"Call me Mallory."

. . .

In Mallory's experience, people had a harder time keeping promises than making them. Like the countless nurses, hovering over her with their needles and assurances that "it won't hurt a bit." Or her parents, who swore she'd be able to live a "normal" teenage life, free from the stares and pointing and behind-the-back whispering.

Rhys Dalton was no exception.

He'd done okay with calling her by her first name. And made an effort to share meals with his son. But more often than not, his busy schedule meant he was called away after a few hurried bites.

In her book, that didn't count for squat.

The situation called for desperate, below-the-belt, borderline-illegal measures. Rhys might be her boss, but her first obligation was to his son. It was time for someone to make him man up and face his parental responsibilities.

It looked like that someone was going to have to be her.

"Ready?" she asked her pint-sized, towheaded accomplice.

Oliver nodded, his expression solemn, like some sort of mini special agent gearing up for a top-secret mission. All he needed to complete the look was a dark suit and a pair of Ray-Bans. "Ready."

"Remember. Your saddest face. It has to be pitiful."

"Pit-ful?" He scrunched up his nose. "What's that mean?"

"Pitiful. It means super sad. A hundred times more than

regular sad." She knelt down in front of him and put her hands on his shoulders. "Can you do it?"

"You bet." He nodded again.

"Show me."

He lowered his eyelids and stuck out his lips in an exaggerated pout. Mallory could have sworn he even blinked back the beginnings of a tear. Kid was a regular Macaulay Culkin.

"Good. If that doesn't get your father to go with us, nothing will." She gave him a high five and stood. "Let's roll."

She grabbed the wicker basket she'd spent the greater part of the morning preparing and shepherded Oliver down the hall to his father's office. They were almost at the door when it swung open and Collins came out.

"Perfect timing." He winked at Mallory and fist-bumped Oliver. She smiled at the not-too-distant memory of how aloof he'd been with her when she first arrived. One taste of her signature version of lemon meringue pie, made with light, flaky sheets of sugared phyllo dough, homemade lemon curd, and a brown sugar meringue, was all it took to break down that barrier. "He's finishing up a video conference."

"You've cleared his schedule for the rest of the day?" she asked, hitching the basket up on her arm.

"All set. Once this teleconference is done, he's free and clear." Collins's eyes darted up and down the hall, and he lowered his voice. "I held up my end of the bargain. What about…?"

"The pie?" she finished for him, not needing to hear the rest of his question. "It's in the refrigerator, cooling for tonight."

Collins smacked his lips, and she jabbed a finger at his chest. "I swear, if so much as a sliver is missing when I come back, that's the last one I'll bake."

"You wouldn't." He stared her down, the slight upward

tilt of his lips undercutting his serious tone.

She stared right back, an equally saucy smile spreading across her face. "I would."

"I'd believe her if I were you," Oliver piped up in solidarity. "She's nice, but strict. She wouldn't let me play video games last night until I brushed my teeth."

"I won't touch it until after dinner. Scout's honor." Collins held up three fingers in the Boy Scout salute and set off to do whatever was next on his undoubtedly long list of daily duties, calling over his shoulder as he went, "Good luck."

The hallway grew eerily silent in his wake. Mallory raised her free hand, poised to knock on the now-closed door.

"Are you okay?" Oliver asked in a stage whisper after a long, awkward moment.

"I'm fine." With both hands occupied, she had to settle for mentally crossing her fingers at the lie. She took a deep breath, willed herself to adopt her sister's no-holds-barred, leap-without-a-net philosophy, and knocked.

"Come in."

Rhys's clipped tone brought her back to their first meeting. Not a memory she particularly wanted to revisit. No one looked fondly back on being fired, even if it was by the first man to make her hormones sit up and take notice since — well, ever. She thought briefly about cutting and running. But he'd heard her knock. It was too late to turn back now.

A tug on her arm made her look down.

"It's okay." Oliver's wide eyes, the same rich shade of brandy brown as his father's, held a wistful, knowing look no almost-five-year-old should possess. "Daddy's not mad. He sounds mad a lot since Mommy died. But he doesn't mean it. He's just sad."

It hadn't taken her long to fall for this sweet, sensitive, lonely little boy who reminded her so much of herself as a child. Both isolated from the world around them, him by an overprotective father, her courtesy of the big C. Her heart swelled, pressing against her ribs until she was sure it would explode.

"How did you get so smart?"

"I dunno." Oliver lifted a bony shoulder. "Mrs. Flannigan says it's because I'm only allowed to watch half an hour of TV a day."

Mallory suppressed a smile. "That must be it."

She reached for the doorknob, her confidence buoyed by Oliver's words—it was true what they said about wisdom coming from of the mouths of babes—but before she could grab it the door swung open and Rhys stood framed in the entryway. She was relieved to see his serious scowl soften the slightest bit at the sight of his son.

"Is something wrong?" His concerned eyes raked Oliver, then her, as if checking for blood or bandages or other obvious signs of distress.

She held up the hamper. "We thought you might like to join us for a picnic."

Okay, so that was a major overstatement. More like she didn't have to be a fortune-teller to predict he'd brush off their invitation, and she had every intention of using every low-down trick in the book to change his mind, up to and including kidnapping.

She gave Oliver a discreet nudge, and his face fell into an expression so forlorn it would have melted even the hardest of hearts.

"Please, Dad? Mallory made your favorite. Fried chicken and potato salad. And I helped peel the potatoes."

Rhys's gaze shifted from his son to her and his scowl reappeared, creasing his forehead. "Is that safe?"

"Under supervision. Oliver's a big help in the kitchen." She laid a hand on her pint-sized sous chef's shoulder. "Aren't you?"

Oliver looked up at her, a crooked grin splitting his face and revealing the gap where he'd lost a tooth that morning. "You bet."

"You lost a tooth," Rhys observed.

"Yep." Oliver proudly poked his tongue through the empty space. "My first one. Mallory says the tooth fairy's going to come tonight, and if I put my tooth under my pillow she'll leave me twenty dollars. We made a special box out of a dollar bill to help her find it."

"Right," Mallory added, jumping on the lost-tooth bandwagon. The kid was a freaking genius. Why hadn't she thought of this angle before? "And we're having a picnic. To celebrate."

"Twenty dollars, huh?" Rhys leaned against the doorframe and crossed his arms over his chest. Mallory tried to ignore the way the sleeves of his polo stretched over his well-formed biceps. "Pretty steep."

She shrugged. "Inflation."

"Well, a lost tooth does sound like cause for celebration," Rhys conceded, looking down at Oliver. His normally steely eyes flashed soft with obvious affection. "Especially your first one."

Mallory's insides did that little flippy thing that seemed to happen whenever Rhys did something to remind her that whatever his failings, he was a man who loved his son. He just needed someone to snap him out of his stupor and remind him that Oliver needed him. Not his money or what it could provide, but him.

Oh. My. God. Her sister was right. Rhys was Captain von Trapp. Cold. Impersonal. Emotionally unavailable. And she was his Fräulein Maria, the sweet, innocent maiden sent to help heal his wounds and make his family whole again.

Except the Straits of Florida would freeze over before he gave her a second glance, never mind fell in love with her.

And no matter what her hula-dancing hormones said, there was no way she was letting herself get involved with him.

No. Way.

"Then you'll come with us?" Oliver's plea snapped her back to reality.

"I'd like to." Rhys averted his eyes, staring down at his loafer-clad feet. Mallory braced herself for the inevitable "but." She didn't have to wait long. "But I have a lot of work to catch up on. Maybe we could celebrate after dinner."

Oliver's lower lip jutted out for real this time, no theatrics required, strengthening Mallory's resolve. "Collins said your schedule's clear for the rest of the afternoon."

"He's in on this, too?" Rhys asked with a smirk.

"Four meals a week," she reminded him under her breath. "You promised. You can catch up on work later."

Rhys glanced over his shoulder, presumably to take stock of the ever-present pile of papers stacked on his desk waiting for his attention. Then he stepped through the doorway and closed the door behind him. "All right, let's go."

"Great." She handed him the basket. "I know the perfect place."

Chapter Six

"Are we there yet?" Oliver piped up for what seemed like the hundredth time from the back of the UTV.

"Almost." It was the same answer Mallory, sitting in the passenger seat of the John Deere Gator next to Rhys, had given the previous ninety-nine times. "It's over that rise."

She pointed a finger at a steep, grassy hill in the distance, and Rhys's worst fears came to fruition. Of all the possible picnic locations on Flamingo Key, what had possessed her to pick that remote spot? How had she even found it? Beth had spent weeks exploring before stumbling upon it.

His foot slipped on the gas pedal, and the UTV lurched.

"Everything okay?" Mallory shot him a concerned side-eye.

He nodded, not trusting himself to speak, and followed her finger, maneuvering the UTV around a stand of cypress trees and toward the base of the hill.

"Hang on to that basket." Mallory half turned in her seat to warn Oliver as they started to climb. "We don't want to lose our lunch."

With her attention switched from him to his son, Rhys breathed a mini sigh of relief. The last thing he wanted was to explain the war of emotions raging inside him. Shock. Pain. Anger. Longing.

Guilt.

His fingers curled around the steering wheel in a white-knuckle grip, and he did his best to concentrate on navigating the uneven terrain. With every inch forward, the invisible weight pressing down on his chest grew heavier, and not because of the treacherous landscape.

As the UTV crested the hill, Rhys braced himself for the rush of memories. Beth, smiling and laughing as she waded in the surf, her long auburn hair blowing in the breeze behind her. Daring him to jump off the outcropping of rocks at the far end of the beach. Holding nine-month-old Oliver's hands as he took his first shaky steps.

Surprisingly, the wave of sentiment that washed over him was more a soft swell than a tsunami, filling him with a quiet, comforting warmth instead of the dull, cold ache he'd expected. Rhys slowed the UTV and took in the scene below him. The sharp slope of the embankment leading down to the small strip of pink-white sand visible at high tide. Beth had pestered him to have a staircase built, but he'd never seemed to have the time. Or make the time, if he was honest with himself. Clear, calm, shallow water perfect for swimming thanks to the protection of the coral reef offshore. A handful of palm trees swaying in the breeze, offering a welcome retreat from the midday sun.

Had he been wrong to stay away for so long? To not share this place with his son?

"It's beautiful." Mallory's half-whispered words reminded him he wasn't alone.

"Are we there?" Oliver bounced in his seat.

"Sit still and hold tight." Rhys glanced back at his son

to make sure he'd followed his instructions. When he was satisfied Oliver was secure, he navigated the UTV down the slope to a shady spot under one of the palm trees.

Oliver jumped down the second the vehicle was stopped. "It's Mommy's beach."

Rhys froze with one leg inside the UTV and one out, his son's words like a roundhouse kick to his gut. Oliver hadn't been two years old when Beth died. There was no way he could remember her bringing him there. "What?"

"Mommy's beach," Oliver repeated. "From the picture."

"What picture?" Rhys asked, his stunned paralysis finally subsided enough for him to climb out of the Gator.

"The one that was in the li-bary." If he hadn't been so shocked and confused, Rhys would have chuckled at his son's mispronunciation. "Mommy's standing in front of that."

Oliver stuck a chubby finger toward the outcropping. "It looks like a duck."

Rhys studied the rock formation at the opposite end of the beach, the one Beth had dared him to jump off. His son was right. If he tilted his head and squinted, it looked sort of like a duck's head, the ledge he'd plunged from jutting out to form the bill. "What do you mean 'was' in the library? Where did it go?"

"Mallory gave it to me. So I could put it on the table next to my bed."

Rhys eyed her questioningly. She had unloaded the UTV and was spreading out a blanket in the shade. She took her sweet time fussing with the thing, kneeling to smooth it down from corner to corner.

When she was finished, she stood and faced him, hands on her slim hips in a don't-fuck-with-me pose. Damn, this woman. He wanted to be mad at her, but at the same time he admired her spunk. "He wanted a picture of his mother in his room. It was the only one I could find."

Oliver had talked about his mother? To someone he'd known for barely a month? If Rhys had needed further proof of how strongly his son had bonded with the new nanny, even after the bee sting incident, this was it.

Icy fingers of regret tiptoed down his spine, making him shiver despite the August heat. He should have been the one Oliver went to if he was curious about his mother. The one to tell him how Beth had never learned to drive because her family moved when she was a teenager to Manhattan, where, according to her, you'd have to be crazy to get behind the wheel. How she'd been strangely fascinated with gummy bears, especially the green ones, which you'd think would taste like lime or sour apple but were strawberry. How she loved to dance around the kitchen with a dish towel, singing the old Rod Stewart tunes her mother had played on repeat.

Rhys shoved his hands into the pockets of the swim trunks Mallory had convinced him to change into before they headed out. When he spoke, his voice was tight. "You should have asked me if you could take it."

She moved the picnic basket onto the blanket, apparently unaffected by his even-shittier-than-usual attitude, and started to unpack. There was the fried chicken and potato salad Oliver promised but also stuffed tomatoes, grilled zucchini, something on skewers, a giant bowl of mixed fruit, and mini mason jars filled with what looked like some sort of pudding and topped with whipped cream, which he assumed were for dessert. The food seemed to keep on coming, like she was Mary freaking Poppins and the hamper was the equivalent of her magic carpetbag.

"You were busy," she said, not bothering to look at him and instead handing one of the skewers to Oliver, who began taking it apart and popping bits of lunch meat, cheese, and olives into his mouth. "Besides, would you have said no?"

Fuck no. Despite what some said about his business

practices, he wasn't completely without compassion. Especially where his son was concerned. But this was no time for weakness, and he wasn't about to admit she was right.

"You've got a lot of nerve for an at-will employee." Rhys claimed a spot on the other side of the blanket and sat.

"Thanks." She beamed at him, and he was struck by the almost unnatural color of her eyes. A brown so pale they were almost gold, with flecks of green around her irises. How was it he hadn't noticed before? "I've been working on my nerve."

"It wasn't supposed to be a compliment." He had to force himself to look away from those unusual, hypnotizing eyes. To distract himself, he grabbed a drumstick and bit into it.

Holy hell. "Delicious" wasn't a good enough word to describe what was happening inside his mouth. The thick, craggy crust crunched between his teeth. Underneath, the meat was moist and tender. A rivulet of juice dribbled past his lips, and he licked it off before it could escape. Was this what he'd been missing out on by hiding in his office, sneaking into the kitchen after mealtime to make himself sad sandwiches?

"Hey," Mallory squealed, breaking him out of his food-induced euphoria. "That's the main course. You can't skip the appetizers."

"It's anti-pasta on a stick." Oliver held up what was left of his skewer proudly. "I made them."

"Antipasto," Mallory corrected, reaching for the drumstick. Rhys pulled it back.

"One more move like that and you're fired." He brought the drumstick back up to his waiting mouth, sank his teeth into the crispy skin, and moaned. "You're going to have to pry this out of my hands with a crowbar."

"You can't fire Mallory." Oliver stepped between them, her tiny self-appointed protector, brandishing his now-empty skewer at Rhys like a sword. "Then who'd make more chicken?"

Busted. Rhys had to hand it to his son. His logic was infallible.

"Put that down." Mallory laid a hand on the boy's forearm and lowered it. "Your father was only kidding. Weren't you?"

The last was directed at him with an arched brow. Rhys nodded. "Of course I was. Now let's eat. The sooner we finish, the sooner we can swim."

• • •

"I'm stuffed." Oliver flopped onto his back and let out a loud burp.

"Say excuse me," Rhys scolded him, spooning the last of his key lime and raspberry pie into his mouth.

Mallory put what little was left of their lunch back into the basket. She'd forgotten how much growing boys could eat. And grown boys, too. Rhys had polished off three— no, four— pieces of chicken by himself. And still had room for dessert. "Burping is considered polite in parts of India, China, and Bahrain. It's a sign of appreciation for being well fed."

"Bahrain?" Rhys licked his spoon, dropped it into his empty mason jar, and handed them to her.

She stowed them away with the rest of the lunch remains and closed up the hamper. "It's a small island nation in the Middle East, south of Kuwait."

"I'm familiar with it. I'm just surprised you are."

Mallory bristled, but Rhys continued before she could go on the attack. "No offense intended. I did some business there, but it's not on most people's radar."

"I'm a classically trained chef." She stood, brushing crumbs off her shorts, and stared down at him. "In case the meal you just wolfed down wasn't enough to jog your memory. I'm familiar with lots of places and their cuisines."

Familiar with, yes. Been there, no. She'd started her independence-fueled rebellion small, sticking to the continental United States. But exploring foreign shores was definitely on her post-cancer bucket list.

Of course, it would be better with a companion. Someone seasoned and well-traveled who could show her the ins and outs of globe-trotting. The best each country could offer. Restaurants. Hotels. Museums.

Added points if he was an attractive billionaire who made her heart race and her toes curl just by looking at her.

Stop it.

"Truce." Said billionaire rose to his feet and extended his hand. "How about we both agree not to jump to conclusions about each other? I won't assume you're not worldly enough to know things like the culinary customs of small island countries, and you won't assume I mean the worst every time I open my mouth."

"I'm plenty worldly. And I do not assume the worst about you." She drew herself up to her full five feet, ready to do battle again, then checked herself.

Damn him, he was right. She was jumping to conclusions, assuming that like her father and mother and everyone back home who knew about her illness, he saw her as a fragile flower, in need of constant protection. Not her usual modus operandi. She was more of a glass-half-full, always-look-on-the-bright-side-of-life kind of girl.

What was it about this man that brought out her inner pit bull? And when had his opinion of her become so important?

She didn't have time to figure it out because Rhys was speaking again, looking at her with a smile that was part snappy comeback, part sexy invitation. "I changed my mind. You're world-wise and urbane."

She regarded him semi-suspiciously, knowing he was only half serious. Still, for Oliver's sake—she swiveled around and was relieved to see he was sitting contentedly cross-legged on the blanket, scraping the sides of his jar with his finger to coax out the last bits of pie—it was best they learn to get along.

After a long minute that felt like an eternity, she took Rhys's outstretched hand and shook it. "Deal."

Big. Mistake. The second their fingers touched something hot and molten sparked inside her, racing down her arm to settle between her legs. She jerked her hand away and took a step back, almost tripping over the picnic basket.

"Your turn, Daddy," Oliver insisted. "You have to burp. Otherwise Mallory will think you don't like her chicken."

Mallory silently praised the powers that be for the impatient interruptions of small children. Oliver's outburst was the cold dose of reality she needed to rein in her raging hormones. As long as he was around, she'd have to keep whatever was going on inside her in check.

Now she just had to make sure he was always around. Shouldn't be much of a problem. It wasn't as if Rhys Dalton was dying to be alone with her. The man did everything in his power to steer clear of her. If there was any way he could avoid her completely, she was 100 percent positive he would.

He proved her point by retreating to the UTV under the pretense of retrieving his sunglasses. "I'm fairly certain Mallory knows how I feel about her chicken. I ate three pieces."

"Four," Mallory corrected. "But who's counting?"

"You, apparently." With his Wayfarers on, she couldn't see his eyes, but she'd bet her mother's Tiffany signature pearl-and-white-gold necklace they were laughing at her.

"Can we go swimming now?" Oliver pleaded, bouncing on the balls of his bare feet.

"Not for another fifteen minutes." Mallory fished a plastic pail and shovel out of her tote bag and held them out to him.

"I think I saw some sea glass over by those rocks." She gestured to the cliff Oliver had recognized earlier, the one he correctly said looked like a duck. "How about we collect some and take it home? We can put it in jars. Or use it to make something, like a picture frame."

"For my mom's picture?" He looked hopefully at his father.

Rhys nodded stiffly. "Sure. If that's what you want."

"Thanks, Dad." Oliver grabbed the pail and raced across the sand, leaving the adults behind without a backward glance. "I'm gonna find all the blue pieces. I like those best."

"So did Beth," Rhys mused under his breath, making Mallory wonder if he realized she was still within earshot. "She said it was the hardest color to find. She loved reverse gems."

"Reverse gems?"

"Traditional gems like diamonds are made by nature and refined by man," Rhys explained. "Sea glass is made by man but refined by nature. That's how Beth liked to describe it."

Mallory stared down at her bare feet, digging her toes into the sand. She'd somehow managed to forget his late wife's tie to the picnic spot she'd chosen. Or deliberately pushed it to the back of her mind.

"I'm sorry for bringing you here." It sounded so inadequate, so hollow, but she couldn't come up with anything more fitting.

Rhys stared down the beach at the distant form of his son, squatting down to sift through the sand and stones. Whether it was because Rhys couldn't or wouldn't look at her, Mallory wasn't sure.

"You had no way of knowing," he said finally, his voice flat and expressionless. Either he had no emotions—which clearly wasn't true from the flashes of warmth she'd seen between him and his son—or he was fighting to keep them under control.

"Oliver figured it out pretty quickly. If I had paid more attention to the picture…"

"The one you stole?"

He turned to face her, and she wished he hadn't. His face was a mix of amusement and angst.

"About that…"

"Stop." He held up a hand. "It was a joke. A bad one."

"No, you're right." She coughed, trying to disguise the crack in her voice. "I shouldn't have taken it without permission. Or forced you to come here. The whole point was to bring you and Oliver closer together. Not stir up painful memories."

"If I'm honest, it wasn't anywhere near as painful as I'd expected it to be. It was more…"

He looked out across the horizon and ran a hand through his windswept hair as he searched for the right word.

"Poignant?" she offered in a half whisper. That was how it felt whenever she visited the hospital where she'd lost so many friends. Sweet and sad and strange.

"Yes, that's it." His shoulders sagged, and he removed his sunglasses to pinch his brow. "Poignant."

His unshuttered eyes found hers, and they shared a moment of profound understanding, one wounded warrior to another. The intensity of their connection shocked her. It was like for that brief sliver of time they shared one breath, one pulse, one heartbeat.

She looked away, breaking the invisible thread between them, and sat down on the blanket, hugging her knees to her chest and staring out at the ocean. "I can see why she loved it here."

Mallory felt rather than saw Rhys take a spot on the blanket next to her. "It was Beth's idea to buy this island. She wanted somewhere for us to relax and unwind as a family, away from the city."

"She sounds like a smart lady."

"Smarter than me in a lot of ways." He stretched out his legs and toed off his Tevas. "I never really appreciated this place until she was gone. Spent too much time worrying about work."

Fighting the temptation to focus on the toned, tanned legs teasing her peripheral vision, Mallory swiveled her head in the direction Oliver had wandered. He sat cross-legged, bucket in one hand and shovel in the other, digging in the sand just above the waterline. Reassured that the son was out of harm's way, Mallory turned her attention back to his father. "You were trying to build a future for your family. There's nothing wrong with that."

"So what's my excuse now?" Rhys lay back, resting on his forearms, and studied the cloudless sky. "Our future is pretty secure."

She followed his example, leaning back on her elbows and gazing upward. "You're here, aren't you? It's a start."

"Only because you practically kidnapped me."

"How you got here isn't important. What matters is that you're spending time with your son." She gestured down the beach toward Oliver.

Rhys closed his eyes and released a long, heavy sigh. "Beth was so much better at this than me."

"At what?" Mallory asked, genuinely confused.

"The fun stuff. She was the hip, cool parent. Picnics. Parties. Playdates. I was the serious, stressed-out one who never learned how to relate to my own child." His eyes opened, shredding her with the hurt she saw in their whiskey-brown depths. "I don't know why I'm telling you all this."

She offered up a hesitant smile. "I'm a good listener."

"No." He grimaced. "I mean yes, you are, but it's not that. I'm not sure why, but I get the feeling you understand me in a way no one has since…"

"Since Beth?" she finished for him, her voice so soft it barely rose over the sound of the waves breaking on the beach.

He was saved from answering by his son, who came running up to them, his bare feet pounding on the sand, a shard of worn glass held aloft in his clenched fist. "Check out what I found. It's got writing on it."

Mallory shared one last look with Rhys, but the moment had passed, for better or worse.

Better, she told herself. *Definitely better.* Whatever strange, psychic current seemed to arc between them, she wasn't going to let herself become a walking cliché. The naive nanny falling for her rich, unattainable boss. She was there for one reason and one reason only. To help put the pieces of this fractured family back together.

Her sister had the wrong Julie Andrews movie. Mallory wasn't Fräulein Maria. She was a modern-day Mary Poppins.

Rhys took the piece of pale green glass from his son and turned it over in his hand.

"What does it say?" Oliver asked.

"It's hard to tell." Rhys ran his thumb over the raised letters. "Looks like it might have been part of an old Coca-Cola bottle. See right here? You can barely make out the *C-O-C*." He handed it back to his son.

"Cool." Oliver held the glass up to the light, squinted at it, then dropped it into his bucket with a hollow *thunk*. "Wanna help me find some more?"

"Sure." Rhys stood and took his son's hand.

"You too," Oliver demanded, waving his bucket at Mallory.

"I think I'll stay here with a good book." Mallory twisted to fish her e-reader out of her beach bag. "You and your dad go ahead. You don't need me tagging along."

Liar, she scolded herself as they walked away hand in hand, the boy a fairer-haired carbon copy of his father. Yes, she wanted Rhys to reconnect with his son. But they could do that with or without her lurking in the background. Truth was, it wasn't Rhys and Oliver who needed space from her.

It was she who needed a healthy distance from the tall, dark, and dangerous one of them.

Chapter Seven

Rhys shut down his computer and pushed his chair away from his desk. Enough was enough, even for a workaholic like him. When the words started swimming on the screen, it was time to call it quits.

He tipped his head back and closed his eyes, enjoying the stillness of the summer night. Late nights and early mornings were his favorite times of day. When the sun was starting to break over the horizon or ending its slow creep downward. When the heat of the day had yet to make an appearance or already abated. When the house was silent, and he could be alone with his thoughts.

In the past, they'd run straight to Beth. Without any danger of discovery, he was free to indulge in his fair share of self-pity and sadness.

But in the last few weeks, another woman had been invading his brain. A petite, amber-eyed blonde with a smart mouth, a quick mind, and a body that would make a monk walk through a sliding glass door.

Yesterday's picnic had only made things ten times worse.

He wasn't the only one who had felt the ripple of electricity between them. And then he'd opened up and spilled his guts like a damn piñata, talking about Beth for the first time in ages, and they'd shared an emotional connection that went beyond the physical. The heightened awareness had them on edge for the rest of their outing.

His stomach rumbled, cutting through the quiet and reminding him the only thing he'd eaten since breakfast was a handful of PEZ from today's Super Mario dispenser. Time to get off his ass and raid the refrigerator. With any luck, a few leftover pieces of Mallory's fried chicken were tucked away on the top shelf behind the orange juice.

He stood, stretched, and made his way to the kitchen. His steps slowed as he got closer. A faint circle of light spilled out into the hallway.

Seemed he wasn't the only one craving a late-night snack.

Rhys checked his watch. Almost eleven. He debated waiting until the coast was clear. But hunger won out over solitude.

When he rounded the corner into the kitchen, he stopped short. A shapely, spandex-clad behind stuck out from the refrigerator, swaying softly from side to side as its owner rummaged through the contents, muttering something about Collins and a missing lemon meringue pie.

Don't stand there and stare at her like an oversexed teenager. Eating is overrated, anyway.

He willed his feet to move.

One step.

She bent lower to reach something on the bottom shelf.

Two steps.

She straightened, balancing a plastic bowl of strawberries against her hip, swung the refrigerator door shut, and turned.

Three.

As if in slow motion, her eyes landed on him and she

screamed. The bowl slipped from her hand, clattering to the floor and sending berries everywhere.

"Sorry." He scrambled to help her pick them up.

She put a hand to her heart and took a ragged breath. "You scared the crap out of me. What are you doing in here so late?"

"The same thing you are." He gestured to the bowl. "Looking for something to eat."

She rescued the last of the strawberries from under the table, dropped them into the bowl, and stood, taking it with her to the sink. "That's what you get for skipping dinner. Again."

He followed her to his feet, pulled the refrigerator open, and peered inside. "Any of that chicken left?"

"Nope." She poured the berries into a colander and turned on the tap, letting the water pour over them. "Your son finished it off at lunch."

"Damn." He sighed and closed the door. "I'm starving."

"Sit." She motioned to the table. "I'll make you something."

"You don't have to do that."

"I know. But I'm a chef. I can't stand to see anyone go hungry. Even someone who couldn't bother to show up for dinner." She shut the water off and popped a strawberry between her plump pink lips.

All the moisture in his mouth seemed to migrate to his palms. He pulled out a chair and sat, if only to hide his reaction to the way her mouth closed over the strawberry, her tongue stealing out to swipe the juice from her lips when she was done. "Go for it."

She wiped her hands on her spandex shorts and crossed back to the refrigerator. "How about an omelet? Or a frittata?"

"Either one sounds great."

She opened the door and studied the contents. "We've got ham, mushrooms, onions, Gruyère..."

"You're the professional." He tipped his chair back and put his hands behind his head. "Surprise me."

She moved with the easy grace of a ballerina, retrieving items from the refrigerator and placing them on a cutting board next to the Keurig. She popped in a K-Cup, stuck a mug underneath, and pressed start before pulling a knife out of a wooden block.

The dance that followed was as intricate as any ballet. Chopping. Scrambling. Pouring. Stirring. Rhys wiped his still-sweaty palms on his khakis, his Adam's apple bobbing in his throat. Who knew cooking could be such a turn-on?

He let the chair fall to the tile floor with a heavy *thud*. Mallory shot him a questioning look over her shoulder, then brought two steaming mugs to the table.

"Milk or sugar?" she asked.

"Neither, thanks." He took a sip. Strong and dark, just the way he liked it.

Mallory turned her attention back to the stove, removing the pan from the heat. She divided her creation between two waiting plates and added a piece of thick bread fresh from the toaster to each.

"Bon appétit." She plunked one of the plates in front of him and sat across the table with the other.

"Thanks." Rhys picked up his fork and dug in.

"Wow." She gaped at him as he shoveled in forkful after forkful, her own utensil stalled halfway to her lips. "You weren't kidding. You really were starving."

"Mmph," he mumbled through a mouthful of the most delicious combination of eggs, meat, cheese, and something he couldn't quite identify that he'd ever tasted. "What's in this?"

"It's classified. I could tell you, but then I'd have to kill you."

Her fork made its way to her mouth, and his hungry eyes watched as it disappeared between her lips.

He cleared his throat. "That would be a shame. Especially when we're starting to get along."

"Are we?" Her tongue darted out to lick her lips clean, and his jaw tightened. The way she ate was as erotic as the way she cooked.

"I thought so."

"You're not still mad at me for giving Oliver his mother's picture?" Her fork hovered over her plate, and she stared at him expectantly.

"I was never mad," he insisted.

She rolled her eyes.

"Well, not for long." He bit into his toast with a satisfying *crunch*. "This is damn good. Beats the hell out of PEZ."

"PEZ?"

"All I've eaten since breakfast. Until this." He took another bite of toast.

She wrinkled her nose. "I didn't know they still made that stuff. Nothing but pure sugar."

He nodded, washing down his toast with a swig of coffee. "My guilty pleasure. A holdover from childhood. It was just me and my mom, and we didn't have a lot. But every Christmas I'd get one in my stocking."

"Where is she now?" Mallory asked, cutting into her omelet.

"She died." Rhys swallowed the lump in his throat along with a mouthful of eggs. Ten years, and it still hurt to remember watching his mother fade away. He'd lost the two most important women in his life, one agonizingly slowly, the other painfully fast. "Cancer."

Mallory's face whitened, and her fork clattered to her plate.

"Are you okay?" he asked.

"I'm fine. Just clumsy." She waved him off, retrieving her fork. Her eyes met his, filled with concern and compassion and something he couldn't put a finger on. "I'm sorry about your mother."

"Thanks." He got the sense she was holding back, but he didn't push the issue, opting to change to a less sensitive subject. "What made you want to be a chef?"

She traded her fork for her coffee cup, some of the color returning to her face. "What made you want to be a tech billionaire?"

"Answering a question with a question." He leaned back in his chair and smiled, relieved that the momentary awkwardness between them seemed to have passed. "Oldest trick in the book. But I'll bite. I didn't set out to get rich. I liked inventing things, and I wanted to make people's lives better."

"I guess you could say the same for me." She sipped her coffee, then studied him over the rim of her cup. "Cooking is creating. Marrying flavors and textures to create something unique and memorable. It's like painting or sculpting, but with food as a medium. And there's nothing more rewarding than planning and preparing a meal that puts food in someone's stomach and a smile on their face."

"When you put it like that, we have a lot in common." He swiped his napkin across his mouth. "We're both innovators and idealists."

"Kindred spirits," she agreed, a pretty blush spreading over her tanned cheeks.

"So why give that all up to come here and play glorified babysitter?"

She shrugged and took another sip of coffee. "I like kids."

"That's obvious from how you are with Oliver." He tossed his napkin next to his plate. "But there must be more to it than that."

"I needed a change." She set down her mug and sighed. "The situation I was in was stifling. I felt like I was being smothered by expectations. Here, I can breathe again. I feel freer."

He crossed his arms over his chest and studied her. It was almost as if he were seeing her for the first time. He'd never considered the courage it must have taken for her to leave everything she'd known and come to a strange place, with strange people, in a new, unfamiliar job. Then he'd gone and made things even more difficult for her by being the world's worst boss. Firing her on the first day. Avoiding her like she was a communicable disease. Not to mention fantasizing about her day and night. Michael Scott from *The Office* had nothing on him.

He stretched out his legs and rubbed the back of his neck. Now was as good a time as any to do something he should have done weeks ago. "I owe you an apology. I accused you of jumping to conclusions, but I'm the one who fired you on sight."

She cocked her head. "I'm sure you had your reasons."

"Stupid ones," he admitted.

"You know what they say." The corners of her mouth curved into a smile. "The first step toward fixing a problem is recognizing you have one."

He leaned forward, resting his elbows on the table. "Does that mean you accept my apology?"

"As long as you accept mine. I should have asked before taking the picture."

She crossed her legs, one turquoise-toenailed foot peeking out from under the table, and his pulse kicked up a notch. They were moving into new, unchartered territory, and he didn't know if he was more thrilled or terrified.

He picked up his fork, speared a bite-sized piece of

omelet from his plate, and held it aloft in a mock toast.

"Agreed."

. . .

"More coffee?" Rhys stood and crossed to the Keurig.

"No, thanks." Mallory put a hand over her mug. "One cup's my limit once the sun sets, or I'd never get to sleep."

"Sleep's overrated." He spun the rack of K-Cups, picked one, and dropped it into the machine.

She focused on her plate under the pretext of finishing her omelet. Anything not to drool over how he filled out his tapered polo shirt and perfectly tailored khakis. Why did he have to be so criminally good-looking? Even overworked and sleep-deprived, he looked like he'd stepped off the pages of *GQ* or *Esquire,* his sexy late-night stubble only adding to his appeal. Throw in his recent attitude adjustment—toward her and his son—and he was damned near irresistible. Her ovaries had practically exploded watching him on the beach with Oliver.

"Let me guess." She scooped the last bit of omelet onto her fork. "You're going back to work. No sleep for the weary."

"Not tonight." He jabbed a finger at the start button and the machine began to whir. "I've worked enough for one day."

"Did I hear that right?" She pushed her chair back and downed the last of her coffee. "The overlord of overtime is calling it a night?"

"There's a first time for everything."

He pulled his mug out from the machine and brought it to his lips. Her traitorous eyes tracked every inch of its journey, lingering on his full, firm mouth as it parted to accept the rich, dark roast. She'd never wished she were a cup of coffee before.

She stacked their empty plates and brought them to the

sink, desperate for something to keep her eyes—and her mind—off his way-too-kissable lips. "I've got to keep up with your son. Sleep's not a luxury. It's a necessity."

"Is that why you were late to breakfast this morning?" He leaned against the counter beside her, his shoulder almost touching hers. Her breath caught and the hairs on her arms stood at attention. "Needed a little extra shut-eye?"

"Not exactly." She bent to load the dishwasher, which had the added benefit of avoiding his gaze. She wasn't about to tell him the truth—that her oncologist had called. And she wasn't about to look him in the face when she lied, especially after he'd been so honest with her about his mother. Cancer. Her whole body had seemed to drop, like she was in a free-falling elevator, when he said the word. "I had some…personal business to take care of."

He surprised her by setting his cup down and helping her with the dishes. Most of the entitled millennials she'd grown up with wouldn't be caught dead doing menial household chores. That was what they had staff for. Once again, Rhys was proving himself to be one giant complicated puzzle. One she wanted more and more every day to solve. "Nothing serious, I hope."

So did she. It wasn't the first time she'd needed to have blood work redone. Labs made mistakes. Samples got tainted or dropped or lost. But Dr. Decker had sounded ominous with his talk of increased white blood cells and abnormal platelets. Or maybe it was her overactive imagination reading into things. He was probably being overcautious.

"No." She crossed the fingers on one hand behind her back and prayed her words would prove to be prophetic. "But I have to go to Key West tomorrow morning."

Dr. Decker had contacted a lab there and arranged to have the necessary tests done. Collins would take her as far as the dock, and she'd Uber it from there. She didn't want to risk anyone finding out where she was going. That would only lead to a whole host of questions she wasn't ready to answer. She liked being plain old never-had-a-life-threatening-disease Mallory Worthington. "Mrs. Flannigan's agreed to watch Oliver until I get back. As long as that's okay with you."

"Of course." Rhys put the last of the dishes in the dishwasher and reclaimed his coffee cup. "You're entitled to reasonable personal time. It's in your contract."

He sounded like a lawyer, all stiff and formal. Like everything else he did, it only made him hotter. The man put the *S-E-X* in sexy.

"Thanks." She hip-checked the dishwasher closed. "I think."

"That came out wrong." He raked a hand through his hair, mussing his usually impeccably styled do. "What I meant to say was you have a right to a personal life outside of work. I'm sure we can manage for a few hours without you."

"Thanks," she said again. This time, it came out like a croak. It was getting harder to form words with him so near. She needed to get out of there before she did something monumentally stupid. Like beg him to bend her over the kitchen counter and have his way with her. "It shouldn't take too long."

"Take whatever time you need." He drained his cup and snaked an arm behind her to deposit it in the sink. His scent—sea and sun mixed with hints of his citrusy cologne —washed over her. "I don't have anything pressing tomorrow. If necessary, I can help Mrs. Flannigan with Oliver. Maybe take him bodysurfing."

"Bodysurfing during business hours?" Mallory kept her tone light, but underneath she was gloating a teeny-tiny bit. "Where's the real Rhys Dalton, and what have you done with him?"

"For a long time, he was sleepwalking through life," he

admitted with a heavy sigh that stirred the hair above her ear. "But he's awake now. Thanks to you."

Heat rose in her cheeks. She grabbed a dish towel off the drying rack and busied herself with wiping her hands. "You just needed a little push in the right direction."

"More than a little push." He chuckled, the low, husky sound rumbling through her like distant thunder on a hot Florida afternoon.

"Okay, then a shove." She folded the dish towel, put it back on the rack, and leaned against the counter, subtly shifting away from Rhys to create some space between them. "But I didn't force you to do anything you wouldn't have done on your own eventually."

"Maybe." He rubbed the back of his neck. "If 'eventually' wasn't too late."

"It's never too late."

"I wish that were true."

His eyes clouded over and grew distant, making it painfully obvious he was thinking of his wife. Or his mother. Or both. He clenched his jaw and let his gaze drop to his feet, his grief so raw it was palpable.

She shouldn't touch him. She should keep a safe distance between them. Say something banal but reassuring, like "they'll always be with you" or "you'll find love again," then follow her initial instincts and run far and fast.

Instead, she made the mistake of looking at him again, and words seemed totally inadequate to ease his suffering.

Against her better judgment, she reached out and put a hand on his forearm. She ignored the unfamiliar tingle that zinged up her arm and settled in her chest. "You're still here. So is Oliver. You have to move forward."

"Easier said than done."

"I know." Almost of its own volition, her hand slid down to his wrist, her fingers twined with his, and she squeezed.

"Survivor's guilt sucks."

His hooded eyes drifted to their joined hands, and he couldn't hide the surprise there. For a second, she thought he was going to cast her off, but while he didn't exactly reciprocate the gesture he let her hand stay where it was, with his limply in her grip. "Who says I feel guilty?"

"Don't you? I do."

The minute the words were out of her mouth, she wanted to yank them back. Since that was impossible, she settled for releasing his hand, picking up a sponge, and wiping down the perfectly clean counter.

Fortunately, he didn't press her. "I guess that explains it."

She stopped wiping to shoot him a puzzled look over her shoulder. "Explains what?"

"Why Oliver took to you so quickly. You understand what he's been through because you've been through it, too."

"So have you," she pointed out, turning to face him.

"It's not the same." His entire body tensed as if he'd been struck by lightning. "Oliver's a child. He's innocent. I'm… not."

She wanted to ask what he meant, but before she could speak he smacked a palm down on the counter, making her jump. "It's late. You should get some sleep."

"Right." She tossed her sponge in the sink.

He moved toward the door without a backward glance, his gait rigid, his arms stiff at his sides. She trailed after him, catching up to him in the hallway, and they walked together in silence to the bottom of the stairs.

"I guess this is where we say good night." Her bedroom, and all the others save the master suite, were on the second floor. The Flannigans lived in the caretaker's cottage, and Collins had a room above the boathouse. Which meant at night the only occupants of the main house were her, Rhys, and a four-year-old who slept so soundly a hurricane wouldn't wake him. Something she tried not to think too much about. She shuffled from one bare foot to the other. "I'll see you in the morning."

"Mallory."

His voice stopped her before she could reach the second step. She spun around to find his posture had softened but his face looked more solemn than ever, if that was possible.

"Thanks for dinner."

His soulful whiskey eyes and smoky nighttime voice turned her legs to gelatin. She grabbed the banister for support. The last thing she wanted was to fall in a lust-addled heap at his feet. The man was still grieving for his wife, not looking to hook up with his nanny. "It was no big deal."

"Yes, it was."

He stepped toward her, the toes of his Top-Siders bumping the base of the stairs. His sunny, salty, citrusy scent surrounded her, and she tightened her grip on the banister. Even one step below her, he towered over her, and she could almost count the unfairly long dark lashes framing his eyes.

"You're welcome." The words came out in a whisper.

Without warning, his head bent, and his lips brushed hers. So soft, so gentle, so fleeting she thought she'd imagined it or entered an alternate universe where smoking-hot billionaire single dads kissed their nannies good night. But then any hint of tentativeness disappeared, and there was no way of denying Rhys Dalton was kissing her like she'd never been kissed before.

Her limited experience with the country club set hadn't prepared her for this. For the sweet slide of his mouth against hers. The flick of his tongue, coaxing her to open for him. The pressure of his fingers gripping her hips, inching her closer.

Heat flared in her belly and spread like melted butter through her veins as he devoured her with a hunger and tenderness that were entirely foreign to her. He made her feel delicious. Desirable.

Daring.

It was all she could do to remain upright. Her hands drifted upward and clutched his hair, his neck, the soft cotton of his shirt—anything to keep from collapsing.

Damn, the man could kiss. He tasted like coffee and Gruyère. She lost all sense of time or place or propriety. Just as she started to relax into him and allow herself to respond, he pulled away. He took one step back, then two, letting his arms fall limp at his sides.

"That was…"

Amazing? Mind-blowing? Life-changing?

"A mistake," he finished. "I'm sorry. It won't happen again. Good night."

He's right, she thought, her glassy, lust-blurred eyes following his retreating form until it disappeared. *You know he's right. It's not like this can go anywhere. The billionaire and the babysitter. It's doomed from the start.*

But knowing that didn't make his words any less painful.

Chapter Eight

"Are you sure this is a good idea?" Mallory handed Collins the cordless drill. "Shouldn't we be evacuating or something?"

Collins looked down from the ladder, where he was putting up the last of the hurricane shutters. "You don't get many tropical storms up north, do you? If we evacuated every time Mother Nature got huffy, we might as well pack our bags and move."

"What about the Flannigans?" She put a screw in his outstretched palm. "They left this morning."

"Preplanned family visit." He loaded the screw into the drill and lined it up with the hole. "It's their granddaughter's first birthday."

"Lucky them." She winced as the drill whined. "Are we almost done?"

"I can finish with this last shutter. Why don't you see if Rhy—Mr. Dalton and Oliver need help with the deck furniture?"

Great. She'd rather eat undercooked pork. But she couldn't admit that to Collins without confessing why. Which would involve telling him about THE KISS. She'd come to think of it like that, in all caps, as if she were shouting internally. A personal, silent scream.

"I thought when we were done here we were going to run into town for supplies."

"I can handle that myself. No need for both of us to be off island." He reloaded the drill, and the whining started up again.

So much for that brilliant plan. She was hoping to sneak over to the lab and see if her test results were in yet. They weren't due for a few days, and Dr. Decker had sworn he'd call as soon as he heard anything. But all that stuff about white blood cells and platelets had her on edge. She wanted to know now so life could either continue as it was, or she'd go back to being Mallory Worthington, poor, sick little rich girl.

The latter was almost too terrible to contemplate. She'd come so far since setting foot on Flamingo Key, and she wasn't talking about the distance she'd traveled from New York. She'd become stronger, more confident, more assertive. She was making her own decisions, living on her own terms. The last thing she wanted was to take a step backward. And that's exactly what would happen if the results showed her cancer had returned. She'd be in another battle for her life, physically and emotionally.

She forced a smile and headed around the back of the house to the deck. There wasn't time to dwell on her health now, not with the more immediate threat of the storm bearing down on them.

"Mallory." Oliver's gleeful shout burst her dream bubble. What was it about a potential natural disaster that got kids so excited? "Come look. We're tying up the chairs, so they don't blow away in the hurricane."

"Hardly a hurricane." Rhys rose like Poseidon from behind a lounge chair, a length of rope in one hand and a pair of kitchen shears in the other. "The forecasters don't think it will be more than a category one by the time it hits land. If that."

Oliver's tiny forehead creased. "Then why are we tying stuff up?"

"Because it's better to be safe than sorry." Mallory dragged herself up the stairs to the deck, each reluctant step bringing her nearer to the man she'd been dancing around for the past week.

"I thought you were helping Collins with the storm shutters." Rhys's eyes were hidden behind his Ray-Bans, his expression unreadable. Her body wanted to close the gap between them and feel his lips on hers again, but her brain cast the deciding when-the-Gulf-of-Mexico-freezes-over vote. Was he as uncomfortable with this whole situation as she was?

Mallory gave herself a mental shake. They had water to freeze and flashlights to find and batteries to check. "He's wrapping things up. He thought you could use an extra pair of hands."

"We're almost done here, too, right, pal?" Rhys gathered up the cushions from one of the chairs and motioned for Oliver to do the same.

"Right." Oliver struggled to collect the bulky cushions. Once he'd managed to corral them, they dwarfed him, his eyes barely visible above the cabana-stripe fabric. Mallory reached out to take one, but he shook his head, his blond bangs flopping wildly. "I got it. Dad says I'm a real good helper."

"The best." Rhys's face was still a mask, but she detected a hint of a smile in his voice that had her insides doing somersaults. Whatever was happening—or not happening— between her and her enigmatic employer, it was obvious Rhys had been making a real effort to repair his relationship with his son, and his effort was paying off.

She grabbed another set of cushions and followed them into the house.

"When we're all ready for the hurricane, can we go watch the waves?" Oliver asked. "The man on TV said they're going to get really big."

"That's what you get for letting him watch the Weather Channel." Mallory hip-checked the door closed, pausing to make sure it clicked securely shut.

"I thought it would be educational," Rhys said, dropping his cushions in one corner of the kitchen.

Mallory bit back a smirk. "Maybe a little too educational."

"Can I?" Oliver asked again.

"Absolutely not." Rhys took the cushions from his son and stacked them with his. "The wind should be picking up soon."

"What about Collins?" Mallory added her cushions to the pile. "He's taking the launch to town for some last-minute supplies."

"He'll be fine." Rhys shrugged off his windbreaker and tossed it over the back of the couch. "If it gets too rough, he'll bunk with one of his bowling buddies."

"If he can go on the boat, why can't I go to Mommy's beach and see the waves?" Oliver whined, throwing in a foot stomp at the last second for extra emphasis.

"Because he's a grown man who knows what he's doing, and you're a four-year-old boy who's not allowed outside without supervision." Rhys unzipped his son's jacket and peeled it off.

"I'm almost five. And you said I was a big boy. So did she." Oliver pointed at Mallory.

If they hadn't been in crisis prep mode, she would have laughed at the standoff. Two peas in a pod. The wide stance. The crossed arms. The stubborn chin.

"I gave you my answer, and my answer is no." The bigger of the two peas narrowed his eyes, not giving an inch. "I don't want you anywhere near that storm surge."

"Your father's right." Mallory jumped in. "We're safest indoors. How about I make some of that white chocolate confetti popcorn you like and we watch a movie on DVD?"

Oliver cocked his head to one side and scrunched up his nose, weighing her offer with a gravity more fitting for a politician than a preschooler. "Can I pick the movie?"

She smiled. "Sure."

"Any one I want?"

"As long as it's rated G."

"*Nemo*," Oliver announced as authoritatively as his four-year-old voice would allow, practically daring her to disagree.

"Again?" They'd seen it at least ten times. She wondered if that had anything to do with the fact that, like him, the title character had no mother and a father who didn't want him to stray too far from home.

He nodded.

"Then *Nemo* it is."

Oliver gave an exaggerated, melodramatic sigh worthy of an Academy Award. "I guess that would be okay."

"Why don't you go upstairs and pick up your room while I make the popcorn? I'll call you when it's ready."

"All right." He started out of the room, then stopped and turned. "But watching *Nemo* won't be as much fun as watching the waves. Even with confetti popcorn."

He clomped out of sight, leaving Mallory to chuckle at his retreating back. "So much for the way to a man's heart being through his stomach."

"I don't know about that." Rhys's throaty baritone sent shivers of desire dancing up and down her spine, reminding her he was still there. And that they were alone for the first time since THE KISS. "I'm pretty sure your fried chicken could stop ships and start wars."

"I'll keep that in mind if I ever want to stop a ship or start a war." She took a covered saucepan from one of the cabinets. No air-popped, cardboard crap for her.

"Thanks for stepping in with Oliver." Rhys pulled out a chair at the kitchen table and sat. She didn't know whether to cheer or curse. Didn't he have something more important to do than watch her pop popcorn?

"The tag team approach. Highly effective." She assembled her ingredients and placed them on the counter next to the commercial stove that was as good as—if not better than—the one she'd cooked on at the Worthington. Peanut oil. Popcorn kernels. Almond bark. Candy sprinkles. "Is there anything else I can do before the storm hits? Make some meals while we've still got power?"

That should keep her mind—and her hands—busy.

"What we've done already is probably overkill." Rhys removed his Ray-Bans and set them down on the table in front of him, revealing those melancholy dark eyes that had the capacity to reduce her to mush. "And the generator will kick in if the power goes out."

"I should have known you'd have thought of everything." The oil crackled in the pan, and she threw in the kernels. "I'll bet you were a Boy Scout."

"Guilty as charged. Got my Eagle in tenth grade."

"That's early, isn't it?" She covered the pan and shook it over the gas flame, the somersaults in her stomach starting to subside. Maybe things between them didn't have to be awkward. Pithy banter she could handle. "Not that I'm surprised. I'll bet you were always an overachiever."

"In some ways," he remarked wryly over the intermittent *pop-pop-pop* of the popcorn. "Not so much in others."

"I can't imagine you being anything other than remarkably adept at everything you attempted."

One dark brow arched toward his hairline. "What about the other night?"

If that wasn't adept, she'd hate to see what was. It would probably leave her in a panting, boneless mound.

The somersaults returned in full force. It was like she had the entire Cirque du Soleil in there. She turned off the burner, letting the popcorn continue to pop, and moved on to melting the almond bark. "If you're fishing for compliments, I thought you did pretty well."

Until he left her hot and bothered.

"I wasn't, but thanks. And the feeling's mutual." For a split second, hope swelled her heart, but his next words sent her crashing back to earth. "But it can't happen again."

She broke the block of bark into pieces and dumped them into a microwave-safe bowl. "Who are you trying to convince? Me or yourself?"

"Both."

She stuck the bowl in the microwave, punching the buttons with more force than necessary. "I hate to sound juvenile, but you started it."

"I ended it, too."

Ouch.

The microwave beeped. She stirred the semi-melted bark and set the timer for another thirty seconds. "I take it back. I've found something you're not adept at. Letting women down easily."

A dark cloud crossed his handsome face. "Beth always said diplomacy wasn't my strong suit."

"It's okay. You're right. You're my boss. I work for you. Kissing you is definitely not part of my job description."

No matter how much she wanted it to be.

The microwave dinged again. She pulled out the bowl of fully melted bark and set it on the counter. "I should get Oliver. He likes to drizzle the chocolate on the popcorn."

"I'll do it." Rhys pushed back his chair and stood. For a moment she thought he was going to say something more. Then, with shake of his head, he retreated, seeming to realize that at least for the time being, she needed the subject of THE KISS to be closed.

As soon as he left the room, the tension seeped from Mallory's body like air from a collapsed soufflé. She busied herself lining a baking sheet with wax paper and spreading out the popcorn. She was almost done when Rhys returned, alone.

"Where's Oliver?"

"I don't know." His face was etched with concern. "He wasn't in his room."

"Did you check the rest of the rooms upstairs?"

"Yes. I can't find him anywhere."

She wiped her hands on a dish towel. "I'll help look. He can't have gone far."

For the next ten minutes, they went floor to floor, searching every corner of the house where a four-year-old could hide and coming up empty.

"We're wasting our time here." Rhys grabbed his windbreaker off the back of the couch and shoved his arms through the sleeves. "He's not in the house."

"You think he went outside?" Mallory cast a cautious eye out the window. The sky had darkened to an ominous gray, and wind whipped the tops of the trees.

"I don't think, I know." Rhys yanked up the zipper on his jacket. "And I've got a pretty good idea where he is."

Their eyes met, and they spoke at the same time.

"Beth's beach."

• • •

The ride to Beth's beach in the UTV was the longest few

minutes of Rhys's life. Longer than when he'd stalked the mailbox checking for grad school acceptances. Longer than the time he'd paced outside the bathroom door of their Tribeca co-op, waiting for Beth to pee on a stick. Even longer than the agonizing moments he'd waited for the doctors to tell him her fate after the terrorist attack two years later.

His son, his lifeblood, the one living soul who depended on Rhys to keep him safe, was out there in the gathering storm, alone, unprotected, and afraid.

He has to be all right. He has to be all right. He has to be all right.

This couldn't be happening again, not after everything he'd done to protect Oliver. He couldn't lose his son now, when they'd just started to find each other.

He floored the gas pedal and the UTV lurched around a stand of trees and up the hill leading to the secluded beach. The air was thick and heavy with moisture. Any second the clouds would let loose, pelting them—and Oliver—with fat, stinging raindrops, soaking their clothes until they felt like lead weights. Already the wind tore through the trees, buffeting the UTV as it made its slow, excruciating ascent. Rhys swore under his breath, willing it to go faster. He punched the gas pedal again, and the UTV swerved.

"Be careful. We're no good to him if we don't get there in one piece."

A light, almost hesitant touch on his knee reminded him he wasn't alone in his blind panic this time. He had Mallory beside him, and if her ashen face and the trembling hand on his leg were anything to go by, she was as fearful for Oliver's safety as he was.

He gave her a tight nod and eased up on the gas. The UTV ground its way to the crest of the hill and began the treacherous trek down as Rhys's eyes frantically scanned the beach below for any sign of his son. Was he there? What if they were wrong and he'd gone somewhere else? Or gotten lost?

"There he is," Mallory shouted over the building roar of the wind and waves.

He followed her pointed finger. Any momentary relief evaporated when he made out the tiny form of his son, crouched on the outcropping he'd thought looked like a duck. He was huddled on the ledge that formed the bill, flattened against the rock face by the force of the wind and the spray of the surf, his pale, thin arms clinging to the cliff.

"Shit." Rhys didn't make any attempt to hide the profanity this time. "How the hell did he get up there?"

"More important, how are we going to get him down?" Mallory asked.

"I've got an idea." He turned the UTV around and gunned it back up the hill.

"Where are you going?"

"To the top of the cliff. I'll have to climb down to him."

In under a minute, Rhys skidded the UTV to a stop and climbed out, leaving the vehicle running and the lights on. A drop of rain splattered on his cheek, and he pulled up the hood of his windbreaker and tightened it around his face, praying the worst of it held off until he had Oliver on firmer ground.

Mallory jumped out after him. "What can I do?"

"There's some rope in the back. Grab it and follow me."

As much as he didn't want to involve Mallory, this rescue was going to take them both. Even then, he wasn't completely confident of their ability to pull Oliver to safety. But they didn't have much choice. It was them or nothing. And nothing wasn't a goddamn option.

Two long strides and he was at the edge of the cliff, bracing himself against a wind gust. He knelt and peered down at his son. Christ, he looked so fragile down there, his small, frail body pressed against the jagged rocks.

Rhys steeled himself to stay calm even as his heart thudded in his rib cage.

"Oliver," he called as loudly as he could, hoping his voice wasn't swallowed by the storm. "Don't move. I'm coming for you."

His son lifted his head, his eyes filled with tears. "Daddy?"

"Don't move," Rhys repeated. "I'll be right there."

Oliver looked down at the churning waves, then back up at Rhys. "I'm scared."

Rhys flinched, his son's thin, frightened wail clawing at his chest, wrapping icy fingers around his heart. "I know you are. Just keep your eyes on me. Don't look down."

Without standing, Rhys turned to Mallory. "Give me one end of the rope and tie the other to the UTV. I'm going to drop it to Oliver and follow it down."

She stared at him. "You can't be serious."

"I don't see what choice I have."

"At least tie it to yourself so you don't fall."

She handed him one end of the rope, her fingers pausing to linger on his, then walked backward with the other to the UTV, where she bent down and attached it to the front axle. He made a loop in his end, slipped it around his waist, and pulled it tight.

"Satisfied?" he asked her.

"Be careful," she said, echoing her earlier sentiment instead of answering him. "Please."

"I will."

She sucked her lower lip into her mouth, and he realized it wasn't only Oliver she was concerned about, it was him.

But right now, he had one objective.

Get. Oliver.

He swung his legs over the side of the cliff. "When I tug on the rope, pull."

Panic flashed in her eyes. "I'm not strong enough to pull both of you up on my own."

"You don't have to. I'll do most of the work. You only have to give us a little extra boost. Can you manage that?"

"I think so." She stood taller against the wind and squared her shoulders. "Yes, I can."

"Good. Wait for my signal." He glanced down to check on Oliver, still huddled on the ledge, his hands white-knuckled on the rocks. "Hang in there, pal. I'm on my way."

He felt with one foot, then the other for a toehold, winding his way down the steep precipice as quickly and efficiently as he could without slipping. The rain had started to fall more steadily, making the stones slick and slowing his progress.

"Hurry," Oliver moaned. "It's hard to hold on."

"Almost there." A few more feet and he'd be able to crowd onto the narrow ledge with his son. "Don't let go."

When his feet touched the ledge, Rhys let out a long, exhausted breath he didn't even realize he'd been holding. He loosened the rope so it was big enough to fit around both of them and slipped it over Oliver's shoulders, turning his son to face him. His pale cheeks were streaked with rain or tears or both. "It's okay. I've got you."

Oliver's lower lip quivered. "Are you mad at me?"

Despite the tight spot they were in, Rhys had to fight not to crack a smile. "We can talk about that later. How about first we get off this cliff?"

"O…okay." Oliver hiccuped.

"Put your arms around me and hold on with everything you've got."

Wordlessly, Oliver complied, wrapping his arms and legs around Rhys's neck and waist. Rhys tugged on the rope, and they began the long climb back up the cliff, made even harder by the increasing wind gusts and the added weight of their now rain-soaked clothing. When, after what seemed like hours, they reached the top, Rhys's arms and legs throbbed with exhaustion. Fortunately, Mallory was there to help them over the edge.

"Take him," Rhys panted before flopping, spent, onto his back on the wet ground. "He's drenched."

"Come on." She freed Oliver from the rope and scooped him up. "I don't know how dry they'll be, but I saw a couple of blankets in the UTV."

Rhys dragged his tired body out of the muck and shuffled after her, then untied the rope from the axle and stuffed it inside his jacket. He started to slide into the driver's seat, but Mallory stood in his way, blocking him.

"You're drenched, too. Take this and wrap yourself up." She thrust a damp wool blanket into his chest. "It's not much, but it's better than nothing."

Numbly, he took the blanket. "Thanks."

"I'll drive. Get in the back with Oliver."

"I can…"

"No, you can't." She gave him a little push toward the rear of the UTV. "You had your chance to play hero. Now it's my turn. Sit with your son. He needs you."

Too tired to argue—and conceding she had a damn good point—Rhys draped the blanket around his shoulders and climbed into the back seat next to Oliver. Mallory revved the engine, and the UTV lumbered down the hill.

His trembling son looked up at him with wide eyes, his fair hair dark with rain and plastered to his face. "Are you going to yell at me now?"

Rhys put his arm around his son, wrapping them both in the blanket. "No, I'm not going to yell at you. But we are going to have a long talk in the morning, once you've dried off, warmed up, and had a good night's sleep."

"I'm sorry I didn't listen to you." Oliver buried his head in Rhys's chest, muffling his words.

"I know." Rhys smoothed a hand over his son's hair.

"Daddy?"

"Yes?"

Oliver lifted his head. "Thanks for rescuing me even though I was bad. I love you."

"I love you, too, buddy." Rhys swallowed hard against the lump in his throat. It had been a hell of a night, one he'd be reliving in his nightmares for weeks. But it had brought them to this point, so at least some good had come from all the pain. "I love you, too."

Chapter Nine

"Is he asleep?" Mallory padded down the hall in pink-and-white striped pajama pants and a matching T-shirt, a towel twisted on top of her head.

Rhys pulled Oliver's door closed. "Out cold."

"All the excitement must have worn him down." She released the towel and shook out her hair, still damp from the shower, assailing him with the coconut scent of her shampoo.

"Not just him." Rhys yawned and slumped against the door. He was mentally and physically fried. The only thing keeping him upright was pure adrenaline, and now that his son was safe, sound, and sleeping, his adrenaline high was starting to wear off.

"Understandable." She used the towel to wring a few final drops from the ends of her long blond waves. "What you did out there tonight…"

"What we did," he corrected. "It was a team effort."

She blushed and ducked her head, hiding her face behind a curtain of damp hair. "I don't know about that."

"I do." He reached up to grab the top of the doorframe,

hoping it would ease the kinks out of his abused and aching muscles. "If you weren't there, who would have pulled us up off that cliff?"

And kept him from falling apart, with her quiet strength and clear thinking.

"You did most of the hard work. I was just there for moral support." She shifted from one prettily polished foot to the other, clearly uncomfortable taking any of the credit for Oliver's rescue. Modesty. Another quality he could add to her long list of attributes.

"Don't sell yourself short. Moral support is invaluable."

"Any word from Collins?" she asked.

Rhys didn't miss the skillful change of subject, but he let it pass, nodding. "He's staying in town with a friend. The storm's moving fast. He should be able to get back sometime tomorrow morning."

"Good. That he's somewhere safe, I mean. And that the storm's not as bad as we thought." Mallory gave her hair one last squeeze and draped the towel around her neck. "I'm going to make myself a cup of tea. Can I get you anything?"

"After the day we've had, I need something a hell of a lot stronger than tea."

"That doesn't sound half bad. If you don't mind sharing."

She stretched, revealing a strip of smooth, tanned skin between the hem of her shirt and the waistband of her pajama pants. The rest of his body might be on the verge of collapse, but his dick had a little life left. He cursed the uncooperative appendage for being so weak-willed and shifted his weight to hide his reaction.

"How about scotch?" he asked. "I've got some eighteen-year-old Macallan."

"I wouldn't know the difference from six-month-old rotgut."

"You will after you taste this."

"If you say so." She gave him a sexy half smile. Tendrils of damp hair clung to her scrubbed-clean face, making her look like a seductive water nymph.

"I need to shower first." Preferably a cold one. "I'll meet you downstairs in a few minutes."

"Sounds good." A gust of wind shook the house, and she winced. "I'll scrounge up some snacks and we can wait out the storm. What goes good with scotch?"

"You're the chef. I'm sure you'll figure out something."

"Challenge accepted."

She turned to go downstairs, and he followed, his eyes tracking the soft sway of her hips in those shouldn't-be-sexy, cock-hardening pajamas. What the fuck was wrong with him? Not four hours ago he'd been clinging to the side of a cliff, fighting for his life and the life of his son. And now he was ogling the nanny.

Again.

When they reached the bottom of the steps, he peeled off and headed to the master suite, going straight for the bathroom and its walk-in shower. He stripped off his clothes, turned the dial to the coldest setting, and stepped in.

Under the harsh, pounding spray, his thoughts drifted invariably back to Mallory. No surprise there. She'd been creeping into his subconscious far too often since that night in the kitchen.

And that kiss.

He braced a hand flat against the tile and swore, letting the icy water wash over him. What the fuck had he been thinking, kissing the damn babysitter? It was a recipe for disaster. If he needed to get laid, he could find any number of willing women on the mainland.

Problem was he didn't just want to get laid. And he didn't want just any willing woman. He wanted Mallory. He wanted late-night chats and early-morning breakfasts. He wanted spontaneous picnics and walks on the beach. Things he hadn't wanted to share with anyone in a hell of a long time.

He looked down to find his disobedient dick at half mast and turned off the shower. Why waste water when it wasn't having the desired effect anyway? He toweled dry, threw on sweatpants and a clean T-shirt, and went in search of Mallory. He found her in the great room, cross-legged on the couch, her face flushed, a half-empty rocks glass in her hand. The bottle of scotch and a second glass sat on the coffee table in front of her, next to a marble cutting board loaded with meat, fruit, cheese, and crackers.

"Sorry." She lifted her glass, whether as a real apology or a mock salute he couldn't tell. "I started without you."

"No need to apologize." He sat on the opposite end of the sofa, not wanting to tempt fate by getting too close to her, then slid the bottle toward himself and poured himself a generous two-finger shot. The rich amber liquid burned a path down his throat to his stomach, taking the edge off his shitshow of a day.

He leaned forward, elbows on his knees, and examined the virtual feast she'd laid out. Was she expecting the offensive line of the Tampa Bay Bucs? "Nice spread."

"If you're half as hungry as I am, there won't be any left when we're done." She cut a slice of some sort of exotic-looking cheese. "Here. Try this. It's Comté. From the French Alps. They mature it in special caves."

She inched next to him, holding the sliver of cheese to his mouth. His brain screamed at him to tell her was allergic to cheese cultures or lactose intolerant. Anything to avoid the intimacy of having her feed him. But instead his lips parted, almost involuntarily, and he closed his eyes as she slipped the sliver into his mouth.

"Good, isn't it?"

Good didn't come close to describing what he was feeling.

She moved closer, so close the hint of scotch on her breath and her coconut shampoo flooded his senses.

"Want some more?"

Oh, yeah. He wanted more.

Eyes still closed, he nodded, his mouth suddenly on strike.

"How about something a little different?" He felt her weight shift forward and heard the scrape of the cutting board as she slid it across the table. "What's your preference? Fruit? Meat? Carbs?"

He had a preference, all right. But it wasn't for fruit, meat, or carbs, and it wasn't one he was going to confess to her. "Surprise me."

"Feeling adventurous?"

He swallowed a groan. "You have no idea."

"Then keep your eyes closed and your mouth open."

The *snick* of the knife on the cutting board was followed by the brush of her fingers on his lips and an explosion of competing flavors on his tongue.

"How does it taste?"

"Rich. Sweet. Creamy." Like he imagined she'd be if he got the chance to taste her again. "What is it?"

"Camembert and truffle honey."

"Sounds expensive."

"It is." Was it his imagination, or had her voice gotten huskier, more carnal? "But it's worth it, don't you think?"

"Definitely."

"What next? I've got some pork rillettes. Or a really nice soppressata."

"Neither." He opened his eyes and took the knife from her unsuspecting fingers. "It's my turn to feed you."

"Okay." She opened her mouth and stared at him expectantly.

His lips curled into the start of a smile. Turnabout was

fair play, and he was going to enjoy teasing her. "Aren't you forgetting something?"

"Like what?"

"Like closing your eyes."

She bit her lip and stared down at the smorgasbord. "How can I be sure you won't put together some terrible flavor combination, like grapefruit and Gorgonzola?"

"You can't." His mouth curved higher. "You'll have to trust me."

She hesitated, then lowered her eyelids.

"Good. No peeking."

He studied the assortment on the cutting board. He had no clue what went with what, or which was the Comté and which was the Camembert. He went by raw instinct, slicing off a piece of warm, soft cheese and topping it with an apple slice.

"Open."

She obeyed, and he lifted his culinary masterpiece to her lips. She took a small, tentative bite, then another, bigger one.

"What's the verdict?"

"Granny Smith apple and Brie. A perfect pairing." She licked her lips, and his brain short-circuited. "You're a natural. Are you sure you don't have experience in the kitchen?"

"Not the kind of experience you're talking about." He dragged his gaze from her way-too-tempting mouth, only to have it land on her chest, the soft swell of her breasts peeking from the V-neck of her pajama top. Not. Helping.

She laughed, the husky, sexy sound making his nerve endings sizzle. "Forget I asked."

He grabbed the knife from the cutting board. "Ready for something else?"

"Why not?" Her lips parted slightly in anticipation.

He hesitated, the knife hovering over a stick of what

looked like some sort of salami. "Any suggestions?"

"You did pretty well on your own last time." She tucked her legs underneath her and sank deeper into the couch cushions. "Trust your instincts."

His instinct was to toss her over his shoulder like a caveman and carry her off to his bedroom, but he was pretty sure that wasn't on the menu. He settled for cutting off a slice of the mystery meat and stacking it on a cracker. He held it up to her mouth, doing his best to avoid contact as she took her first nibble.

"How's that?" he asked, his voice strangled, choked with desire. He shouldn't want her. It was wrong on every level. He was her employer. He should slam on the brakes, walk— no, run—away, at least until they had a chance to talk about whatever was happening between them. But none of that logic topped the tsunami of sexual energy flooding his body.

"Soppressata on a classic Club cracker. Simple, but delicious." She opened her mouth for another taste, letting out a little moan when he fed her the rest.

"Still hungry?" he asked when she finished.

"Starving."

She licked her lips again. Christ, he wished she would stop doing that. It wasn't fair to expect a man to control himself faced with that kind of invitation.

He cleared his throat. "What else would you like to try?"

She opened her eyes, and he was struck by the heat he saw in their depths. One hand crept out to rest on his thigh, like she was afraid to scare him off. It stopped just short of the now obvious bulge in his sweats, her eyes never leaving his.

"You."

• • •

Mallory had clearly lost her mind.

Or maybe it was crouching on a cliff in the middle of a near hurricane while two people she cared about battled death and the elements on a narrow ledge a few feet below that had her throwing caution to the wind and propositioning her boss. Either way, there was no turning back now. Not that she wanted to, not with the evidence of her effect on him inches from her hand.

He pried her fingers off his thigh, and a wave of mortification threatened to drown her. His body might be saying yes, but it looked like his brain was screaming *not in this lifetime*. What had she been thinking? Taking a job hundreds of miles from home, in a place she'd never been, working for a man she'd never met, doing a job she was hugely overqualified for was one kind of crazy. Hitting on her billionaire boss was another.

She retreated to the opposite end of the couch and pulled her knees up to her chest. "Oh my God, I'm so sorry. I don't know what I was thinking. I mean, I know what I was thinking, but obviously it's not what you're thinking even though I thought we were thinking the same thing."

"Mallory." If she'd thought her name sounded like sin on his lips before, now it was pure sex, fueled by the late hour, lack of sleep, and good scotch.

"Yes?"

"Stop talking."

"I can't help it. When I get nervous or embarrassed I babble, and right now I think I'm more nervous and embarrassed than I've been in my entire…"

In one swift move, he was over her, his hands in her hair and his mouth on hers, swallowing her words in the most delicious way imaginable. She was too stunned to protest even if she wanted to—which she so did not. She was done fighting this thing, and it looked like—finally—he was, too.

She moaned into his mouth and rocked her hips, more turned on than she'd ever been. Her hands left her sides to explore his neck, his shoulders, the swell of his biceps as his arms wound around her back.

The lights flickered and went out, and she stiffened. In the pitch darkness, the wind and rain seemed to batter the house even harder.

"It's okay," Rhys whispered against her lips, his strong arms banding tighter, pinning her to him. "Give it a few seconds. The generator will kick in."

"Oliver…"

"Is fine." Rhys's mouth moved to her cheek, then her jaw, then her neck, leaving kisses—and goose bumps—in its wake. "Fast asleep, I'm sure."

The lights flickered back on. She threaded her hands in his hair as his mouth slid lower still. "Maybe that was a sign."

"Of what?" He nipped the delicate skin at the hollow where her neck met her shoulder.

She let her head fall back, loving the delicious incongruity of his full, soft lips and rough stubble on her fevered flesh. She was starving, desperate for him. "That we shouldn't do this."

"But we're going to, aren't we?" It sounded more like a statement than a question, as if their lovemaking was a done deal.

"I can't stop myself," she admitted, breathless. "I don't want to."

"Neither do I."

His lips returned to hers, and they gave in to the desire that had been swirling between them for weeks. Her skin sizzled. Her stomach flip-flopped. He heated her from the inside out, turning her into a molten mass of want.

Without warning, he broke off and stood, taking her with him.

She wrapped her arms and legs around him and squeezed

tight. "What are you doing?"

"Not here," he growled, moving toward the one hall in the house she'd never gone down—the one that led to the master bedroom. "Our first time is not going to be on my goddamn living room couch."

Our first time. Her heart leaped. She'd been trying to live in the moment and push aside all her worries about the morning after. Knowing he wasn't thinking about this as one-and-done made that a lot easier.

"Oh."

If Rhys was disappointed in her anemic response, he didn't show it. He dropped kisses on her forehead, eyelids, even the sensitive shell of her ear as he shouldered his way through the bedroom door and hit the light switch, casting a warm yellow glow. He stopped next to the bed and let her slide down his body. She felt every hard edge and smooth curve of him, making her already racing heart pound faster.

His busy fingers grabbed the hem of her T-shirt and lifted it up. Not one to stand in the way of anything that would facilitate a little skin-on-skin action, she raised her arms over her head, allowing him to pull it off. His hungry gaze raked her too-small chest and slightly rounded belly.

She moved to cover herself, but he stopped her, his hands closing around her wrists. "Don't. You're perfect. Better."

"Than what?" she asked, half afraid for the answer.

"Than I imagined."

He released her hands, and they fluttered to her sides. "You imagined this?"

"So many times." His voice was deep and gravelly, and his chest rose and fell with each labored breath. "You have no idea."

"I think I do." It was her turn to rake him from head to toe. He had way too much clothing on, and she mentally willed him to take off his shirt, so they'd be on even footing.

"I imagined you, too."

"Fuck, Mallory." His hands tore through his hair. "You can't say things like that."

She blinked up at him. "Why not?"

"Because now I can't help but picture you lying in your bed upstairs, touching yourself while you thought of me." He slid one hand up her thigh to the opening between her legs, rubbing her through the light cotton of her pajamas. "Did you?"

"Yes," she whispered. She ducked her head to hide the flush she could feel creeping up her cheeks.

"Don't," he said again. "Don't be self-conscious."

He tipped her chin up with a finger, forcing her to look at him as his other hand continued to tease her. "Do you know what I did after we kissed the other night?"

"No." The word came out on a moan.

"I went to my room and took a long, cold shower. And when that didn't work, I jacked off. I was hoping it would get you out of my system."

"Did it work?"

"Fuck no." He replaced his hand with his rock-hard erection, lifting her leg and hooking it around his back. "Does it feel like it worked?"

"Fuck no," she echoed, making him chuckle.

His eyes darkened, and he ducked his head to murmur low and seductive in her ear. "Then how about we put ourselves out of our misery?"

He didn't wait for an answer, laying her on the bed and following her down. Somewhere along the way, he managed to strip off his shirt and sweats, leaving him in only a pair of form-fitting boxer briefs.

Christ, he was beautiful. Even seeing him on the beach in those running shorts hadn't prepared her for this. For him, all firm muscle and tight skin, up close and personal. Chest to chest. Hip to hip. Thigh to thigh.

"Need you naked." His hands trailed down her sides, over her rib cage, to the waistband of her pajama pants, igniting a string of sparks.

Mallory lifted her hips for him to slide them off, and they went the way of her top. She reached out a tentative finger to touch the bulge under his boxers, then pulled it back. "Now you."

He took her hand and brought it back to his groin. "Only if you return the favor."

She inhaled deeply and held her breath, trying to stop her hands from shaking as she hooked her thumbs in the elastic of his boxers and began to slide them down. His skin was superheated, scorching the tips of her fingers, and she sucked in a gasp when he sprang free from his spandex prison, stiff and pulsing, smooth skin stretched tight over rigid flesh. She froze midthigh, her hands still clutching his waistband.

"Don't stop now. Not when it's just getting interesting."

He sounded as hungry for her as she was for him. The thought that she'd brought him to this point—drowning in need, drunk with desire—thrilled her and made her bold. She inched his boxers down his legs to his ankles. "If you ask me, things got interesting when you went all caveman and carried me off to your bedroom."

He kicked his boxers the rest of the way off and pulled her against him, aligning their bodies so she could feel every glorious ridge and valley of him. "If you found that interesting, you're going to love what's next."

Flipping her onto her back, he covered her with his weight, his strong arms anchored above her. Her eyes flickered from his chiseled abs, to his powerful chest, to his broad shoulders, finally landing on his lips. Swollen and shining from their kisses, they curved into a smile that slayed her. When he looked at her like that, she was a goner.

"Are you going to kiss me?" she asked, returning his smile tenfold. "Or stare at me all night?"

His grin got even bigger, and she fell even further. "As much as I like looking at you, I'm going to have to go with option A."

He skimmed his lips down her neck, leaving hot, openmouthed kisses behind her ear, on her jaw, and on the curve of her cleavage that had her panting and clawing at his back. She silently begged him to continue his journey to her nipple, but instead he retraced his path, wrapping a hand in her hair to anchor her head as he took her mouth, his lips moving forcefully, assuredly on hers. She opened to him, and he accepted the invitation, deepening the kiss as his free hand wandered over her body, skimming her breast, her waist, her hip. Arching her back, she rocked her wet center against his erection, showing him where she wanted him most. "Shit. Condom." He rolled away from her and stood. "I think I've got a couple in here somewhere."

He disappeared into the master bath, and she could hear him rummaging through the cabinets.

"You think? You mean you're not sure?" She grabbed a pillow and clutched it to her chest, not bothering to try to hide her disappointment.

"Sex hasn't exactly been a priority for me lately."

The drawer slamming continued for a few minutes, and Mallory had just about lost hope when Rhys came striding out of the bathroom with all the confidence and swagger of a knight who'd slain a dragon. A very naked, very aroused knight holding two foil packets aloft in one hand. "Success."

He ripped one open with his teeth and slid it on, tossing the other onto the nightstand. It was a first for her, openly staring as her lover suited up, and she was fascinated by his movements. The ease with which he held himself. The confident way he pinched the top of the condom, slipped it on, and rolled it down, smoothing it over each inch of his hard length.

"Enjoying the view?"

Her cheeks warmed and she and looked away. The intricate pattern on the geometric rug was fascinating...

"Hey." His voice, low but urgent, drew her eyes back to him. She tried to keep her gaze above the waistline this time. "A man likes to be admired. And to admire."

He gestured to the pillow.

She released her death grip, letting it fall in slow motion to the floor.

"That's more like it."

He stood, gloriously exposed in the middle of the room wearing only a condom, and studied her. His eyes danced with a sexy sort of mischief as they raked her up and down, sending prickles of anticipation racing across her skin. After a long minute, he joined her on the bed, covering her body with his and making every inch of her aware of every inch of him. "Are you ready?"

She loved that he asked. That he didn't plunge right in without making sure she was mentally prepared for what they were about to do. Like he realized what a huge leap they were taking and wanted to make sure they were both all in, holding hands as they stepped off the cliff.

But they couldn't stop now. They'd already left solid ground and were in free fall.

She licked her lips and nodded.

He sank inside her and started to move, slowly at first, then faster. Her lips parted and she moaned as he filled her again and again. A shiver ran down her spine as she took it all in. This man. This night. Their intense connection.

She closed her eyes and buried her head in his shoulder, inhaling his spicy, sweaty scent.

He stopped thrusting, creating a whole new set of

sensations. "Too much?"

"No." She breathed in again, loving the feel of him stiff and stationary inside her. If anything, it wasn't enough. She was afraid it would never be enough.

He lowered himself to his elbows and pushed into her, teasing, shallow thrusts that had her whole body humming like a live electrical wire.

She hitched one leg around his waist and moved against him, meeting his rhythm.

He picked up the pace, and her other leg joined the first, crossing at the ankles.

"Rhys." His name slipped out as she drew him deeper, digger her fingernails into his back.

He pressed his lips to her jaw. Almost without thinking, she let her head fall back, giving him free rein over her neck, shoulders, and breasts, his wandering mouth finally finding her nipple. That was all it took to push her over the edge into oblivion, shattering beneath him. Rhys wasn't far behind, groaning her name as he climaxed.

He rested his forehead on hers, and they waited for the tremors to subside. After a few minutes of blissful, postorgasmic togetherness, he rolled off her and headed for the bathroom to dispose of the condom. She started to sit up, not sure what she was supposed to do. Go? Stay? Join him in the bathroom and suggest they share a shower?

He returned before she could figure it out.

"Going somewhere?"

She shook her head, her sex-mussed hair swirling around her face and almost obscuring her view. "Not unless you want me to."

"I don't." He slipped onto the bed behind her, spooning his chest to her back. He threw a leg over her hips, and she could feel his hardening length nudging the cleft between her butt cheeks.

"Are you…?"

"Yep," he said proudly, nipping her neck.

"Already?"

"What can I say?" One hand came around her waist and curled upward to cup her breast. "You're good for my powers of restoration."

"So…" She hissed when his thumb brushed her nipple. Even that slight contact was enough to make it pebble. Apparently, her restorative powers were strong, too. "Does that mean you're good to go again?"

"I've created a monster." His laughter ruffled the hair behind her ear. "What am I going to do with you?"

She rested her head on his shoulder and closed her eyes, letting herself revel in his touch. "I'm sure you'll come up with something."

Chapter Ten

The house was strangely quiet when Rhys woke the next morning.

And that wasn't the only thing that was strange.

When he tried to move, a soft, warm weight held him down. A weight that smelled of summer rain and freshly washed sheets and coconut shampoo.

He stared at the ceiling and waited for the guilt to come crashing down on him like a ten-ton truck. But instead he felt…right. At peace.

Should he feel guilty for not feeling guilty? Rhys turned his head to study the woman sleeping beside him, her fucked-all-night blond curls splayed out across her pillow and a satisfied smile gracing her beautiful face. Six orgasms would do that to a girl. Or was it seven? He'd lost track. After they'd used up their meager supply of condoms, he'd had to resort to more creative tactics to get her off.

He craned his neck to check the digital clock on the nightstand. It was six. Oliver wouldn't be awake for another hour, at least. Maybe two after the ordeal he'd been through yesterday. Plenty of time for another go-round with the warm, willing woman next to him.

He ran a hand down Mallory's spine, his fingertips grazing her skin. She moaned and stirred.

"Good morning." He rolled over and pressed his chest to her back, kissing the nape of her neck.

She groaned louder and buried her face in her pillow.

"Not a morning person, huh?" He reached around to stroke her stomach. "I'll bet I can change that."

"I love mornings. Usually." She arched into him, letting her head fall back on his shoulder. "But someone kept me up all night."

"I didn't hear any complaints." His hand wandered lower, to her already-wet sex. He loved how responsive she was for him. There was nothing deceptive about this woman. She was too open, too transparent to hide what she was feeling.

"Point taken." Her body tensed, and she put a hand over his stopping him. "What time is it? Oliver..."

"Won't be up for at least another hour. Which gives us plenty of time for round four. Or is it five?"

"What if Collins comes back?"

"We'll hear the boat." Rhys bent his head and sucked her earlobe into his mouth. "Any other objections?"

"I can't think of any." She removed her hand.

"Then be quiet and let me touch you." He slipped a finger inside her. Her muscles clenched around him, and he smothered a groan in her neck.

"Be quiet?" Her legs opened wider, and he added a second finger as he continued to work her over, his pace fast enough to tease but not to take the edge off.

"Strike that. I love the noises you make. Be as loud as you want."

"What about you?"

"I'll be as loud as I want, too."

"That's not what I meant. You're taking care of me. What about you? Don't you want to—"

She bit her lip and frowned, searching for the right word.

"Are you trying to ask how I'm going to reach the big O?"

"Well, we're out of condoms."

"Something I'll have to fix soon." How, he didn't have a fucking clue. He didn't go into town all that often. And it wasn't like he was going to ask Collins to get them. Or have Mrs. Flannigan add them to her grocery list. "But that didn't stop us last night, did it?"

Mallory burrowed into her pillow again, shielding her face, but not before he caught a glimpse of the rosy flush creeping up her neck.

"I have an idea." He eased his fingers out of her, eliciting a frustrated groan from her pouty lips. "Turn around and straddle me."

"Why?"

"For once, trust me and follow instructions."

She did, and he gripped her hips, helping to position her over his mouth.

"You're not going to—?"

"Oh yes, I am." He proved his point by curling his hands around her ass and lifting his head to give her a quick, teasing swipe. "And so are you."

He lowered her to him, and for the next ten minutes—okay, maybe it was more like twenty—they explored each other thoroughly, completely, with lips and teeth and tongues, bringing each other to the brink and back, again and again. It was all he could do to hold off until she tensed above him, calling out his name.

When she stopped trembling with the aftershocks of her orgasm, he rolled her off him. "I'm almost there."

She curled her fingers around his length, bringing him back to her mouth. "Then be quiet and let me finish."

"Be quiet?" he teased.

"Never mind. Make as much noise as you want."

He did, not holding anything back, letting her know with each gasp and moan how much he liked what she was doing to him until he let loose. He didn't know what was more satisfying, his own release or the way she came apart on top of him. He pressed a kiss to her inner thigh, and reversed positions so they were face-to-face, gathering her sweat-dampened, deliciously naked body to his side. She sighed and twined a leg around one of his, sliding the arch of her foot up his calf. A flash of fluorescent orange caught his eye, and he smiled.

"Can I ask you a personal question?"

"After what we just did?" She snaked a hand up between them to caress his chest, her nails lightly scraping over his nipple and making him jerk. "How can I say no?"

Her foot slid higher, and he reached down to grab her ankle. "What's with the nail polish?"

She glanced up at him with wide, confused eyes. "What do you mean?"

"I'm no expert, but it seems like you wear a different color every other day. Do all woman do that?"

"I don't know about all women, just me. Pedicures are my guilty pleasure. Like PEZ is for you. I match the names to my mood."

He stroked her instep with his thumb. "What's this one called?"

She looked away, her wild, après-sex hair shielding her face. "I don't remember."

"Liar." He rolled them over so he was on top of her and hooked a finger under her chin, tilting it up and forcing her to look at him again. "Come on. You can tell me."

"What if I don't want to?"

"I thought you said there was nothing I couldn't ask." He

brushed a lock of hair off her cheek and kissed her.

"I didn't say I'd answer."

"I'll torture you into submission." His mouth moved lower, tracing a wet trail to the valley between her breasts.

She moaned. "I'm not sure this counts as torture. Isn't it supposed to be cruel and inhuman?"

"It will be when I stop."

"Okay, okay. I give in." She clutched his head to her chest. "It's called A Roll in the Hague."

"Interesting." He laughed against her skin. "So, either you're looking to get laid or you're planning a trip to the Netherlands."

"I've always wanted to go to the tulip festival, but that's in the spring."

"Then I guess you'll have to settle for this."

He drew one nipple into his mouth and flicked it with his tongue, gearing up for another round, when the patter of little feet came racing down the hall.

"Daddy? Are you up? I can't find Mallory."

"Shit." She pushed him off her and scrambled to sit, clutching the sheet around her gorgeous breasts.

"Relax." He gave her a quick kiss, jumped out of bed faster than his exhausted body should have been able to, and yanked on a pair of board shorts. "I've got this. I'll get him some breakfast and take him outside to survey whatever damage there is from the storm. That should give you time to shower and get dressed."

"Thanks." She relaxed her grip on the sheet, and it slipped down a fraction of an inch, giving him a tantalizing glimpse of one creamy mound.

He commanded his libido, which had a mind of its own, to calm the fuck down and went for the door. He and Mallory had a lot to figure out.

But first he had to head off the impressionable four-year-old only seconds away from discovering them.

• • •

"Are you all right? I knew it was a bad idea for you to go down there."

Her mother's voice dripped with disapproval, and Mallory instantly regretted calling her. The hurricane-that-almost-was-but-wasn't had been all over the news for days, and her guilty conscience wouldn't let her rest until she let her parents know she was safe. But a quick text would have done the trick. And she could have deleted her mother's snarky responses without reading them.

She tightened the belt on her robe and grabbed a brush to run through her freshly showered hair. "I'm fine, Mom. The storm turned out to be nothing."

"Hurricanes and alligators—who needs that?" Mallory could almost hear her mother shudder over the phone line. "When are you coming home?"

"This is my home." Mallory answered reflexively, but for the first time in a long time the words didn't feel like a lie. Had she landed where she truly belonged? Found her place? Her purpose?

Her person?

She gave herself a mental shake. No. Her feeling of belonging wasn't because she and Rhys were doing…whatever it was they were doing. It was Oliver, Collins, the Flannigans, all of them. In the short time she'd spent on Flamingo Key, they'd become like family to her.

"You know what I mean." Pamela Sinclair Worthington was formidable when she was angry, and it was clear from her tone she was well on her way to royally pissed off. "You belong here, in New York, with us. Living in the guesthouse. Working at the Worthington. Not cooking, cleaning, and caring for some troglodyte and his spoiled son."

Troglodyte? Who talked like that? The next time Mallory called her mother—if there was a next time—she'd be sure to have a dictionary handy.

"I don't clean." Mallory sat at her vanity and ran the brush aimlessly through her hair. "We have a housekeeper for that. And Oliver's not spoiled. He's a nice, normal four-year-old boy." Who'd been through a lot for a little kid, something Mallory could relate to. But she wasn't getting into that with her mother. The last thing she needed was a reminder of her daughter's medical history.

She sighed and stared at her reflection in the mirror. Flushed cheeks. Bee-stung lips. Tender breasts, her still-sensitive nipples clearly visible through the silk of her robe. She looked like a woman who'd been well and thoroughly shagged. Was it that obvious? Would Collins take one look at her when he got back and know what she and Rhys had done the night before? And that morning?

What about Oliver? He was young but perceptive. Would he figure out something was different?

"Are you still there?" Even traveling via radio waves from hundreds of miles away, her mother's shrill tone could pierce Mallory's ears. And her heart. "You're deliberately avoiding the question."

Mallory stuck the brush under her arm and switched the phone to her other ear. "What was that again?"

"You know perfectly well what I said." Her mother practically spat out the words. Mallory swore she could feel spittle fly through the airwaves. "When are you going to give up this ridiculous charade and come home?"

With more calm than she felt, Mallory grabbed the brush and began tackling the hair on the other side of her head. She'd been spared her parents' disapproval growing up thanks to her cancer and later because she'd played the dutiful daughter, going along with their plans for her without objection. Was this what Brooke had been dealing with all these years? How did she do it without resorting to physical violence? Mallory had new respect for her as-of-yet-non-homicidal sister.

"I know Dad doesn't get it, but I thought you understood why I had to leave. I need to be on my own for a change, without you and Dad always there to catch me when I fall."

"That was before your life was in danger in that swamp you're calling home. I almost lost you once. I'm not going through that again. I can't."

Her mother's voice broke on the last word, making Mallory feel like crap. But like her therapist said, as difficult as it had been for her parents to see her in a hospital bed, hooked up to tubes and monitors, it was wrong for them to use her illness to hold her hostage.

Not that she needed her parents to make her feel like a prisoner of her disease when she had reminders like the test results she was waiting on, hanging over her head like a guillotine.

She laid down the brush and stood. "I know my being sick was hard on you and Dad. But you can't keep me in a bubble forever."

"Why not?" Her mother sniffled. "It worked for John Travolta in that TV movie."

Mallory went into the bedroom and flopped down on the bed. Why did talking with her mother have to be so exhausting? "Actually, it didn't. In the end, he fell in love and left the bubble, deciding to take his chances in the outside world."

"That's right. I always hated that movie."

Mallory punched her pillow in frustration. "I'm a grown woman. You have to let me live my life."

"I'm trying," her mother said, sounding sincere. "But it's

hard adjusting to this new you. My sweet, docile Mallory has become stubborn and headstrong. You're acting like..."

"Like Brooke?" Mallory offered.

"Yes, if you must know." Her mother huffed. "Is this your sister's influence? Did she put you up to this?"

"No, she didn't. This is about me, Mom. Not Brooke."

"I was hoping the storm made you reconsider your decision to move."

"New York has weather, too. Blizzards. Nor'easters."

The line went silent for what seemed like forever but was probably less than a minute. Mallory was starting to think her mother had hung up on her when the older woman finally spoke. "Well, I expect you home for your sister's reception next month. She might have eloped, but that doesn't mean we can't celebrate with a few hundred of our closest friends."

As if her mother cared about celebrating. The whole thing was a thinly veiled vehicle for her to show off Brooke's Fortune 500 bridegroom to all her high-society friends. The fact that Brooke would be miserable for the entire event was an added bonus, punishment for her daughter's decision to run off and get married without her.

But that was Brooke's problem, not Mallory's. She closed her eyes and relaxed into her pulverized pillow. It looked like her mother had given up the come-home-where-we-can-control-you battle. For now. Mallory had no illusions the war was over. "Of course. I've already asked for the time off and booked my flight."

"That's a small consolation, I suppose."

"Let me know if there's anything I can do to help with the arrangements."

"From all the way down there? Doubtful." Ah, the disdain was back in full force. "But I appreciate the offer."

On that not-so-high note, Mallory bade her mother a ck goodbye and clicked off. Her next call to Brooke was a completely different minefield. She'd always had a hard time hiding anything from her sister. One little slip, and Brooke would know every detail of Mallory's recently rediscovered sex life.

She steeled her voice to remain as neutral as humanly possible. Her sister picked up on the first ring. "Hey, Brooke. How's things in the big city?"

"It's about time you called and let me know you're okay." Her sister sounded only moderately less annoyed than her mother. "You are okay, aren't you?"

"It hasn't even been twenty-four hours. And everyone's fine here."

"Everyone, huh?" Brooke's raised eyebrow was almost audible. "Does that include Captain von Dreamy?"

Mallory bristled. "I wish you'd stop calling him that."

"Oh. My. God." Brooke squealed. Actually squealed. Mallory didn't think she'd ever heard that particularly nauseating sound come out of her normally sarcastic sister. "You went all Fräulein Maria on his sexy ass, didn't you?"

"I did what?" Mallory bolted upright.

"You slept with him, you dirty girl. I'm so proud of you."

What the actual fudge? Was her sister psychic or something? Mallory had no idea what she'd said to give Brooke the admittedly correct notion she and Rhys had sex, but she wasn't about to give her any more ammunition. "I don't remember that in the movie."

"It's implied." The distinctive crinkle of a candy wrapper told Mallory her sister had broken into her ever-present stash of junk food. "And you didn't deny it. So how was it? Is he as good in the sack as he looks?"

Mallory gritted her teeth. "I'm not discussing this with you."

"That's funny," Brooke mumbled through a mouthful of what Mallory assumed was her sister's chocolate of choice, a

Milky Way. "I remember you grilling me about Eli."

"And I remember you refusing to answer."

"Just tell me you're going to do it again. Or should I say do him again? And again, and again, and again…"

The thought made Mallory shiver in anticipation. "He's my boss."

"That didn't stop Maria."

"You're not going to let this whole *Sound of Music* thing go, are you?"

"I only want to see you happy," Brooke insisted. "After everything you've been through, no one deserves that more than you."

Mallory's voice softened. "I know your heart's in the right place. And I am happy. Really. For the first time in my life, I'm where I want to be, doing what I want to do."

"Or who you want to do."

"Stop. Seriously." Mallory's wry laugh took some of the bite from her words.

"Fine. I'll let it drop for the time being. But don't think this conversation is over."

"We'll see about that." Mallory stretched her legs out in front of her and yawned. She'd almost forgotten how tired she was. The price she had to pay for a night of wall-banging sex and hardly any sleep. "You know, you'd better be careful. You're starting to sound like Mom."

It was Brooke's turn to chuckle. "Heaven forbid."

The unmistakable sound of an outboard engine cut across her sister's words. Collins was back.

"I have to get going." Mallory swung her legs over the side of the bed and stood, crossing to her dresser. "I'll see you in a few weeks for your post-elopement gala."

Brooke groaned. "Don't remind me. Mom is driving me crazy with invitations and seating charts and flower arrangements."

"It'll all be over soon." Mallory riffled through her drawers, pulling out underwear, a tank top, and a pair of denim shorts. "Then you and Eli can live peacefully ever after."

"From your lips to Mom's ears. She's so beside herself that I landed one of Manhattan's most eligible bachelors, I'm afraid she'll never leave us alone. Especially now that you're hundreds of miles away."

"Trying to guilt me into moving back home?" Mallory shrugged off her robe and stepped into her panties. "Now you really do sound like Mom."

"No. But you know what would get her off my back?"

"What?" The bra was next, followed by her shirt and shorts.

"If you found your own most eligible bachelor. Say one with a private island, a tech fortune, and a penchant for naughty nannies. Extra points if he's got a cute kid she can go all grandmotherly on."

"It's official." Mallory buttoned her shorts and slipped her feet into a pair of vinyl flip-flops. "The transformation is complete. You don't just sound like Mom, you are Mom. Although I can't imagine anyone describing her as grandmotherly."

"You wound me." Brooke's tone was more playful than hurt. "Now go get your man."

"He's not..."

But Brooke had already hung up. And Mallory wasn't sure how convincing her response would have been anyway.

Chapter Eleven

Rhys's stomach rumbled, and he checked the time on his computer screen. Almost noon. He usually skipped lunch, which Mallory constantly warned him wasn't healthy, but for some reason today he was ravenous. Probably in no small part due to their marathon sex session the night before, this one even longer—and wilder—thanks to the lock he'd installed on his bedroom door and the value pack of Trojans he'd ordered from Amazon Prime.

Remembering made him hot, made him want to do it all over again—and more. He adjusted himself beneath the zipper of his khakis and saved the spreadsheet he was working on. Now he needed food and a cold shower, not necessarily in that order.

A knock interrupted his thoughts. Without waiting for a response, Collins pushed through the door, a plate piled high with pickles, potato salad, and the thickest sandwich Rhys had ever seen in one hand and a glass of what looked like sweet tea in the other.

"Mallory thought you might want a little snack." Collins

set the food and drink down on the desk.

It was almost spooky the way she anticipated his needs, in and out of the bedroom. If he dwelled on it too long it would freak him the fuck out, so he didn't, choosing to focus instead on the plate of food in front of him.

"Looks like more than a little snack." Rhys sat down and took a bite of the sandwich. Corned beef on rye, exactly the way he liked it with melted swiss and a dab of mustard. He washed it down with a generous slug of tea. "Delicious. Thank her for me."

"You can thank her yourself when you see her." Collins crossed his arms over his chest and eyed Rhys. "Which you seem to be doing a lot more of recently."

Rhys returned his assistant's stare over the rim of his glass. Yes, he and Mallory had been spending more time together in the days—and nights—since the storm. But they were discreet. He thought. "If you have something to say, then say it. You've never been good at beating around the bush."

"Mrs. Flannigan saw her coming out of your room this morning."

Fuck.

"Yes." Collins took a seat in one of the guest chairs with a smirk. "That's what we suspected."

Rhys's chest tightened, and he smashed a fist on his thigh under the cover of his desk. "I didn't mean to say that out loud."

"Is there something you want to tell me?" Collins asked, adding a mocking eyebrow raise to the smirk.

"Like what?" Rhys pushed his plate away, his appetite gone. "You seem to think you know everything already."

"I wouldn't say everything." Collins leaned back calmly in his chair, his unruffled demeanor only infuriating Rhys more. This conversation called for a drink. Something way stronger than sweet tea.

Rhys stood and went to the bar cart. "It's your fault I'm in this mess."

"My fault?"

"You're the one who convinced me not to send her packing." Rhys's hand shook, sloshing Macallan onto the bar cart. He topped off his drink and tossed it back, draining the scotch in one long gulp that burned a trail down his throat to his stomach. "This is exactly what I was afraid would happen."

"Afraid you'd sleep with her?" Collins prodded. "Or afraid someone would find out?"

Rhys sighed. In all honestly, he couldn't say he regretted having sex with Mallory. But he would have preferred to keep their nighttime activities on the down-low, for her sake as well as his.

"If it makes any difference, I, for one, heartily approve," Collins said, jutting his chin out like a damned peacock. "Why do you think I wanted her to stay? I had a feeling about you two."

Rhys poured himself another generous portion of scotch and slumped back down at his desk. "I don't remember expanding your job duties to include matchmaker. "

"You might not have, but someone else did." Collins reached into his jacket, pulled out a plain white envelope, and pushed it across the desk to Rhys.

Rhys started at it like it was laced with ricin. "What's this?"

"A letter."

"I can see that." Rhys frowned, still not moving to pick up the envelope. "Who is it from?"

Collins rose and crossed to the bar cart. He picked up a bottle of Maker's Mark. "Mind if I help myself?"

"Answer the damn question."

"I'll take that as a no." Collins poured himself two fingers of bourbon.

"Are you going to tell me who the letter is from or not?"

Collins leaned against the paneled wall and sipped. "Beth."

Rhys recoiled like someone had slapped him. "I don't understand. Why do you have a letter from my wife?"

"Do you remember how sick she was during her pregnancy?"

"Of course." She'd been diagnosed with preeclampsia, putting both her and the baby at risk. Rhys had thought his troubles were over when Oliver was delivered without incident.

"She had a lot of time to think about her own mortality while she was on bed rest." Collins resumed his seat and took another nip of bourbon. "She worried about what would happen to you without her. She wrote letters for you and the baby and left them with me. Oliver will get his on his eighteenth birthday. She asked me to give you yours when you met someone new."

Beth had pictured him with someone new? Ironic she'd been able to when it had been impossible for him.

Until recently.

Rhys picked up the envelope between his thumb and index finger. "And you think that's Mallory?"

"I think she's the closest you've come in three years."

For the first time, Rhys studied the envelope. His name was scrawled across the front in Beth's distinctive, flowery script. He traced her handwriting with one finger. "Why didn't you give the letters back to Beth after Oliver was born?"

"I tried. She didn't want them. Said nothing had changed and I should give them to you both if anything happened to her." Collins finished off his bourbon. "It was almost like she knew her time on earth was short."

"She never said anything like that to me." Rhys flipped the envelope over and fingered the flap.

"She wouldn't, would she?" Collins stood and returned his empty glass to the bar cart. "I'll let you read it in peace. Call me if you need anything."

He stopped at the door, his hand on the knob, and turned. "And Rhys?"

"Yes?" Rhys looked up from the sliver of white in his hand.

"For what it's worth, I'm not the only one who approves of you and Mallory. We all agree she's good for you."

"Who said I needed anyone's approval?"

"No one," Collins admitted. "But you have it anyway. You're different with her here. Working less. Spending more time with your son. You seem happy for the first time in a long time."

He turned back to the door for a second, then spun around, pointing a finger at Rhys. "Don't mess it up."

With that parting shot, Collins was gone, leaving Rhys alone with his thoughts and Beth's letter. He turned it over in his hands for a few long minutes before he worked up enough courage to slide his index finger under the flap and rip it open.

His palms damp and his throat dry, he pulled out a single sheet of notebook paper—no fancy stationary for his always-practical Beth—and read.

My dearest Rhys,

If you're reading this, it means I'm no longer with you, and you've met someone new, someone you can see yourself sharing your life with.

I'm glad. Really and truly, I am. I don't expect or want you to live like a monk. I'd be a lousy wife if I wanted that kind of life for you.

And I think I was a good wife, wasn't I?

Anyway, I know if you've judged her worthy of your love she must be caring and compassionate. I hope she makes you laugh and reminds you to eat three square meals a day and take time off from work to stop and smell the sunshine. I hope whatever happened to me that our child is with you and that your new partner loves him or her as much as I did, and I know you do.

I want you to know I have no regrets. Our life together may have been short, but every moment I had with you was a blessing. Yes, even the ones when you forgot to put the toilet seat down or snored so loudly you kept me up all night. True love and soul mates do exist, and I was unbelievably lucky to spend over a decade with the love of my life and my best friend.

Be happy. Be healthy. Be good. Don't be afraid to love again. And don't forget that every day matters. Make them count.

See you on the other side.

All my love always,
Beth

Rhys let the letter flutter to the desk, his vision blurred by tears. He reached blindly for his scotch and slugged it down, swallowing hard against the lump in his throat.

Leave it to Beth to find a way to smack him upside the head, even in death.

• • •

"Where's Dad?" Oliver whined. "I want him to put me to bed tonight."

"Who am I, nobody?" Mallory joked, struggling to hide the doubt niggling inside her head and her heart. Truth was, she had no idea where Rhys was or what he was doing. For the first time in almost a week, he'd barricaded himself in his office, not even coming out for dinner. "I thought you liked me."

"I do," Oliver said, taking his Spider-Man pajamas from Mallory's outstretched hand and pulling them on. "But Dad always forgets to make me brush my teeth, and you never do."

Right. Priorities. She took Oliver by the shoulders, turned him toward his bathroom, and gave him little push. "Go. Brush. Then I'll read you another chapter of *Mrs. Piggle-Wiggle*."

"With the voices?" he asked.

She smiled. "Yes, with the voices."

An hour later, Oliver had been tucked in and read to, and Mallory was in her room with a glass of sauvignon blanc and the newest Sophie Kinsella on her e-reader. She closed the book after reading the same sentence three times, opened the sliding glass door, and stepped out onto the balcony.

She leaned on the railing, her wineglass dangling between two fingers, and looked out over the horizon. The sun hung low, a red-orange ball suspended over the gentle swells of the Atlantic. She tried to concentrate on the beauty and serenity of the scene in front of her and not on the churning in her belly.

She was becoming "that" kind of girl, and she hated it. Needy, clingy, demanding. Freaking out because Rhys changed up their routine. They hadn't made any promises. He had every right to some alone time. Her head told her it was healthy for them to spend time apart.

Unfortunately, her heart couldn't seem to grasp that concept.

She sipped her wine as the last of the sun disappeared.

This was getting out of control. She was working for him. Sleeping with him. And now, she feared, falling in love with him.

To make things even more complicated, she didn't have the results of her blood tests yet. She'd missed a call from Dr. Decker's office earlier. His nurse left a message for her to call back, but by the time she'd seen the notification on her cell phone, the office was closed for the day. Mallory had listened to it over and over. *Your results are in, the doctor would like to speak to you, please call back at your earliest convenience.* Short and succinct, not much to go on. Although that hadn't stopped her from trying in vain to read between the lines.

"Beautiful view."

Rhys's deep, gruff voice made Mallory almost drop her glass onto the patio below. She turned slowly to face the man who occupied a disproportionate number of her waking thoughts, her stupid heart racing when she caught sight of him.

Why did he always have to look so good? He'd traded the button-down shirt and khakis he typically wore during business hours for a pair of cargo shorts and a white polo that set off his tanned skin. His hair was disheveled and his eyes hooded, but none of that detracted from the pull he had on her whenever he was in her general vicinity.

She shivered despite the still-warm September night air, his presence a welcome distraction from worrying about something she couldn't control. She'd get her results tomorrow and face the consequences—whatever they may or may not be—then. Tonight, she was going to live in the here and now. "The sunsets are spectacular in the Keys."

"I wasn't talking about the sunset." He leaned on the rail next to her, and she detected the faint smell of scotch on his breath.

She ignored the compliment and went back to studying

the horizon, the twilight sky now streaked with red and orange. "I didn't hear you come in."

"The door was open."

"I...we missed you tonight. At dinner, I mean." There she went again. Needy, clingy, and demanding.

Fortunately, Rhys didn't notice. He was focused on something else, namely her ass, which he was fondling through the lightweight cotton of her sleep shirt. "I had some things to work through."

"Is everything all right?"

His hand slipped under her nightdress, her skimpy lace panties the only thing that stood between her bare skin and his probing fingers. One of those fingers toyed with the elastic around her thigh, sliding underneath then retreating, teasing her. "It is now."

Her breath hitched, and she almost dropped the glass again. "Wh-what are you doing?"

"If you have to ask, I'm not doing it right." With his free hand, he took the glass from her fingers and set it down beside him.

"Out here?"

He tensed, then withdrew his hand from under her nightgown, leaving her hot and wet and aching for more. "No."

He scooped her up, one arm under her knees and the other around her back, and cradled her to his chest as he carried her into the bedroom. He nuzzled her hair off her neck, dropping a lingering kiss on the spot where her shoulder met her collarbone before laying her tenderly on the bed.

Slowly, agonizingly, he undressed her, taking his time to map every inch of skin he exposed with his fingers and tongue, making her breath come in ragged gasps. When he was done, he stood and stripped for her, and she let her eyes feast on him.

His eyes shone soft and warm, the evening breeze had tossed his hair into a sexy, ruffled mess, and she'd never wanted him more. This wasn't hard-core sex. It wasn't some casual hookup. It was something altogether different and far more frightening, their connection so acute it was almost painful.

She reached out for him, begging without words. He bent down to pull a condom from the pocket of his shorts, ripped it open, and rolled it down over himself. Then he rejoined her on the bed, gently pushing her back against the pillows.

"Feel what you do to me?" He took her hand and laid it flat against his chest. The rapid staccato of his heartbeat under her palm almost matched hers. "Here."

He moved her hand lower, between his thighs. "And here."

Words couldn't describe the torrent of emotions whirling inside her, so she didn't bother to try. Instead she kissed him, without hurry, without pressure, without uneasiness about the future or dwelling on the past. This kiss was slow, thoughtful, controlled. Two people with all the time in the world to touch, to taste, to bask in each other's body.

When they had stoked the heat between them from an ember to an inferno, he entered her with torturous slowness. The slick sounds of their lovemaking mingled with the gentle lapping of the surf, the two rhythms matching and becoming one. She was torn between wanting the sweet sensations to go on forever and desperately needing release. She held on as long as she could until she lost control, opening her mouth in a silent scream as she spasmed around him. He went next, grunting out his orgasm, his cries echoing into the still night.

Gradually, his movements slowed. She coiled herself around him like she might float away if she wasn't anchored to something—to someone. He rested his chin on her head and they lay there like that, spent and sated, until their breathing slowed and their heartbeats returned to normal.

"I know my timing sucks," he said finally, his breath stirring her hair. "But I've got some bad news."

"You're not dumping me, are you?" she teased, planting a kiss in the center of his sweat-slicked chest.

"No." He brushed a lock of hair from her cheek, his hand remaining to cup the back of her head. "But you might want to dump me."

"Not likely."

The hand at the back of her head tangled in her hair, massaging the nape of her neck. "Collins and the Flannigans know."

"Know what?"

"About us."

"What?" She pushed against his chest, but he held firm, his arms tightening around her like steel bands.

"Relax."

"How?"

"Take deep breaths and let your muscles go limp."

"No, I mean how did they find out?"

"Mrs. Flannigan saw you leaving my room this morning."

Heat flooded her face. "How am I ever going to face her?"

"If it makes you feel any better, we have their approval." He stroked her back, warm tingles following the path of his hand. "They think you're good for me."

"How can you be so calm?" She tried to pull away again. He loosened his hold slightly but kept her close. "Everyone knows I'm screwing the boss."

Even as she said it, the word tasted wrong in her mouth. Sharp. Bitter.

"This." He waved a hand between them. "What we just did. That was not screwing."

"Then what are we doing?" she whispered.

"I'm not sure," he admitted.

"I thought...I mean, I assumed you wanted to keep things casual." Time seemed to stop while she waited for his answer.

"Maybe at first." He pulled her closer and brushed a light kiss across her lips, and her doubts started to slowly dissolve. "But not anymore."

Her heart swelled with hope, but her rational brain still wasn't convinced. "Why the sudden shift?"

His eyes shuttered for a second. "I got a wake-up call."

She bit her lip. "I don't understand."

"I'll tell you all about it later." He yawned and kissed her again, this time longer and harder. "Right now, we could both use some sleep."

"Here? she asked, her lips still buzzing from the desperate pressure of his mouth on hers. "What about Oliver? He's across the hall."

"I'll set an alarm and be out before he wakes up."

Mallory gave up the losing battle and snuggled into him, letting her head rest on his chest. "Okay."

They hadn't settled anything. She didn't have a clue where their relationship was headed.

But her heart didn't seem to care.

Chapter Twelve

Rhys had a new favorite hobby.

Watching Mallory sleep.

Bordering on creepy stalker? Maybe. But that wasn't stopping him from taking advantage of the rare opportunity to study her openly, unobserved.

She lay in his arms, her breathing deep and even. No makeup. Hair strewn all over her pillow, a few stray strands stuck to her cheek. Kiss-swollen lips slightly parted, an occasional soft snore escaping between them.

Christ, even her snoring was adorable.

Yeah, he wasn't just verging on creepy stalker. He'd crossed the border into Christian Grey territory.

He would have continued staring at her until the alarm on her cell phone went off, but nature was calling. He tore his eyes away from the object of his obsession and eased his way out of her embrace. He was halfway to the bathroom when a sharp, high-pitched scream split the heavy summer night air.

Oliver.

Rhys went into crisis mode, scrambling for his long-ago-discarded clothes, but Mallory, who'd been dead to the world seconds before, somehow got the jump on him. She threw on shorts and a T-shirt and was out the door before he had one leg in his boxers.

Another scream had him moving triple time. He raced barefoot across the hall to Oliver's bedroom, skidding to a stop inside the doorway. Mallory was seated on the bed with Oliver cradled in her arms, rocking him back and forth and crooning. Moonlight streaming in through the slats of the blinds bathed them in streaks of silver.

"Shh." She stroked Oliver's hair, plastered to his damp forehead. "It's only a nightmare."

Oliver lifted his pale, tearstained face. "Mommy?"

Mallory's shoulders stiffened, the movement so slight it was barely perceptible, but she didn't correct him. "It's okay. I'm here."

Rhys's gut twisted, his son's one-word plea a dagger through his heart. He was adult enough to know it was totally normal for a child to call for his mother. And that it was pointless for Mallory to correct Oliver. But that didn't make it any easier on his psyche.

"Is there anything I can do?" He hated feeling so goddamn helpless. Out on the cliff, he had a purpose. Getting his son to safety. Something to push his fear to the back of his mind and force him to take action. Now all he could do was stand, paralyzed, while Oliver kicked and thrashed, his reddish-brown eyes wide open but seeing nothing.

As if on cue, Oliver's eyelids drooped, and he went limp in Mallory's arms. She laid him down and pulled the blanket up to his chest.

"Is he okay?" Rhys asked, keeping his voice low.

"Night terror," she explained, smoothing Oliver's hair back. "Has he had them before?"

"No." Rhys took a tentative step into the room. "Not that

I'm aware of."

"He'll be fine." She stood and bent to adjust the blanket.

"Did you see what I saw? He was terrified."

Mallory stroked Oliver's cheek and straightened. "Trust me, he won't remember any of it in the morning. It was more frightening for you than it was for him."

As scared as he'd been, Rhys found that hard to believe. He'd seen the terror in his son's eyes. But for Oliver's sake, he hoped Mallory was right. "How do you know so much about this stuff? Don't tell me you're a sleep specialist and a chef?"

"Hardly. I used to have night terrors when I was Oliver's age, but I grew out of them. I'm sure he will, too." Mallory glanced back at Oliver, his blanket rising and falling with each rhythmic inhale and exhale, and lowered her voice. "Let's talk outside."

Rhys nodded. Mallory followed him into the hall and closed the door behind her, making sure not to let the latch click.

"About what Oliver said in there…" Her voice trailed off.

"When he called you 'Mommy'?" Rhys winced at the last word. It wasn't one he'd heard much in the past three years, and it conjured images of Oliver and Beth together, images that were both hurtful and heartwarming.

"It didn't mean anything." Mallory stared up at him, her eyes begging him to believe her.

"I know."

"He was dreaming," she insisted. "He had no idea what he was saying."

"I know."

"I'm not trying to replace his mother. I'd never do that."

Of course she wouldn't. Sure, it was a punch in the gut to hear his son mistake Mallory for Beth, but Rhys didn't think for one minute it was something Mallory encouraged or even wanted.

Words weren't going to convince her he understood, but maybe actions would. He stepped closer, backing her against the wall. She blinked, surprised, as he ducked his head and captured her mouth, silencing her. Her lips parted on a sigh and she pushed up on tiptoe, snaking her arms around his neck and pressing her soft breasts against his chest.

He meant the kiss to be gentle, reassuring. But her more-than-enthusiastic response shot that plan to hell, and within seconds it turned hot and hungry. They kissed like teenagers, their hands roaming but never slipping under their scant clothing.

She pulled away, biting her lip in that adorable way that always made him hard. "It's almost five. I should get some sleep before sunrise. And you should go back downstairs before Oliver wakes up again."

She was right. But that didn't mean he had to like it.

He let his arms fall and took a step back. "See you at breakfast?"

She raised one foot to scratch the back of her leg. She'd changed her nail polish again, this time to a neon green. "If you can pry yourself away from your work."

"I will if you make that French toast Oliver likes so much."

"Oliver?" One arched brow lifted further.

He held his hands up, palms out, in a gesture of defeat. "Okay, me. Although in my defense, Oliver's a big fan, too."

"Since you put it that way, sure."

He gave her one last kiss and headed down the hall, forgetting until he was at the bottom of the stairs that he'd left the rest of his clothes in her room. He thought about going back for them, then shrugged it off. It wasn't like what he and Mallory were doing was a secret from anyone but Oliver.

If their relationship was going to continue—and he hoped to hell it was—that would have to change. As would the fact that he was paying Mallory to work for him during the day and sleeping with her at night.

The arrangement left a bad taste in his mouth. He meant what he told Mallory. This wasn't just fucking for him. For the first time in a long time he wanted something more, a real connection with someone who shared not only his bed but his hopes, his dreams, his life.

A connection that sounded a lot like love.

The unexpected appearance of the L-word made him stop short. Was that where he and Mallory were headed? He'd only loved one woman in his life. After Beth's death, he never imagined he could love again.

But Beth had. She not only imagined it, she hoped for it. She hadn't wanted him to spend the rest of his life alone and in mourning.

It was too much for his sleep-deprived brain to process. He yawned and raked a hand through his bedhead. His mattress was calling to him. Maybe after some shut-eye the answer to his dilemma would miraculously appear.

• • •

"Mail for you, dear." Mrs. Flannigan held out a thin white envelope to Mallory as she entered the kitchen.

Mallory stretched and yawned, the effects of another late night of bedroom gymnastics compounded by Oliver's night terror still catching up to her. She took the envelope and set it down next to the Keurig. Whatever it was, it could wait until she got her morning caffeine injection. She took a mug from the rack next to the machine, stuck it under the dispenser, popped a K-Cup into the basket, and hit the start button. "Thanks."

"I couldn't help but notice the return address," the housekeeper mused as she stood at the counter, continuing to sort through the rest of the mail. "I hope nothing is wrong."

Mallory glanced down at the envelope. Her heart skipped a beat when she recognized the logo for Heritage Labs.

Her blood test results. They'd gotten pushed to the back of her brain by the next-level sex and Oliver's night terror. Not that she could ever really forget she was a cancer survivor. It was an invisible badge stamped on her soul that branded her as indelibly as Hester Prynne's scarlet *A*.

But it had been nice to pretend to be normal for a while.

"Aren't you going to open it?" Mrs. Flannigan prodded.

"It's nothing," Mallory lied, snatching up the envelope and stuffing it into the back pocket of her capris. "Some routine blood work for my annual physical."

The housekeeper eyed Mallory over the top of the Williams Sonoma catalog she was leafing through. "You're not pregnant, are you?"

Mallory had to swallow fast to keep from spitting out her first sip of coffee.

"Um, no," she said when she'd recovered. "No chance of that."

"Are you sure?" Mrs. Flannigan asked, setting the catalog down and focusing all of her attention on Mallory.

"Yes, I'm sure." More than sure. She and Rhys had used protection religiously. Even without it, her chances of getting pregnant, while not nonexistent, were less than optimal, a side effect of chemotherapy and another reminder of the toll cancer had taken on her body.

Which was why that one word from Oliver—"Mommy"—had been like a dose of cold, hard reality. As much as she'd grown to care for him, she wasn't his mommy, and she might never be anyone's mommy. That was something she'd learned to accept. But what about Rhys? He said he wanted more than a physical relationship. Would he still want that when she told him the truth?

"Pity." The housekeeper sighed, thankfully interrupting Mallory's somber stream of thought before she drowned in self-pity. "This house could use the pitter-patter of more little feet. And Oliver could do with a younger brother or sister. Although I suppose it would be best if you and Mr. Dalton got married first."

Married? This time Mallory couldn't stop herself from spewing coffee all over her shirt.

"Now, Millie," Mr. Flannigan scolded, walking through the door with an armful of groceries. "I thought we agreed not to meddle in the young folks' love life."

Young folks? Mallory couldn't remember the last time she'd heard that phrase. If ever. She traded her coffee mug for a napkin and dabbed at her stained shirt.

Mrs. Flannigan took the bags from her husband and put them on the counter. "You agreed. I crossed my fingers behind my back."

"Remember what happened the last time you tried to play matchmaker?" He fished an apple out of one of the bags and bit into it.

"They got married, didn't they?"

"And divorced three years later."

Mrs. Flannigan ignored her husband and began pulling out groceries and lining them up on the counter for inspection. "Did you get the baker's yeast?"

"Was it on the list?"

"Yes."

"Then I got it."

"Let me take care of that," Mallory said, stepping in between them. "I'm sure you have plenty of other chores on your to-do list."

"Well…" Mrs. Flannigan hesitated. "The laundry's overflowing. I should get that started."

"Go." Mallory shouldered the housekeeper out of the

way and reached into one of the bags. "I'll finish up here and start breakfast."

"Thank you, dear."

"Don't mind Millie," Mr. Flannigan half whispered so his retreating wife wouldn't overhear. "She means well. After everything Mr. Dalton's been through, she wants to see him happy. We all do. And you make him the happiest he's been in years."

"I wish I were as sure of that as you are," Mallory admitted, the words spilling out of her mouth before she could stop them.

"Don't sell yourself short. Millie and I have worked for Mr. Dalton for more than six years. Ever since he and his late wife bought this place. For the first time since her death, his days are more than working, eating, and sleeping. He's living again. Smiling. Laughing. Playing with his son. And that's all because of you."

Mallory emptied the last of the groceries from the bags and started stowing the perishables in the refrigerator. "You give me an awful lot of credit."

"You deserve it. But it comes with a lot of responsibility. Letting someone in—trusting again, loving again—is a big step for him. Don't make him regret it."

The caretaker gave her a polite nod that told her he'd said his piece and headed off in the opposite direction of his wife, crunching his apple as he went. Mallory let his words sink in as he disappeared.

Rhys said it himself last night. This thing between them wasn't casual. And it wasn't only their hearts on the line. Oliver had a lot to lose, too.

With a weary sigh, she closed the refrigerator door and leaned against it. It was time to come clean. She and Rhys were already in too deep. He deserved to know about her medical history and all the baggage that dragged along with it.

But first she had to know her test results. She pulled the envelope from her back pocket and tore it open, quick and dirty, like ripping off a Band-Aid. She took out the single sheet of paper inside and unfolded it, letting the envelope float to the floor.

White blood cell count—normal. Red blood cell count—normal. Platelets, proteins, sugar, electrolytes, enzymes—all normal.

Mallory let out the breath she didn't realize she'd been holding and slumped down to the floor, her back resting against the cool stainless steel of the refrigerator. She drew her knees up and hugged them to her chest, not bothering to wipe away the lone, relieved tear streaming down her cheek. She'd dodged another bullet. But there would be more. Her life was a series of scares. There was always the chance she'd have a late recurrence or second cancer.

Rhys had already lost one wife. And his mother, to cancer no less. He had a right to know the risk he was taking getting involved with her.

If she could only figure out how to tell him.

Chapter Thirteen

"I'm bored," Oliver whined, swinging his stubby legs. Cookie crumbs dotted his pouting lips. "I want to go to the beach."

Mallory pulled out the chair across from him and sat. "I told you, it's too damp out. Today is an inside day. We can play Chutes and Ladders. Or build a blanket fort."

Oliver wrinkled his nose. "We did that yesterday. And played freeze dance and put on a puppet show and melted all my broken crayons in a muffin tin to make new ones. We're running out of inside stuff to do."

He might be only four, but she couldn't argue with his logic. It had been raining on and off for three days, and they'd almost exhausted her mental catalog of indoor activities.

"Do you need anything in town?" Collins asked, striding into the kitchen and grabbing a banana from a basket on the counter. "I have to deliver some documents for Mr. Dalton."

Mallory's stupid heart skipped a beat at Rhys's name. He was closing some big deal, and she hadn't seen much of him in the past few days except for the odd meal with Oliver and their clandestine late-night rendezvous. Which explained why she hadn't told him about her cancer. She couldn't say anything in front of Oliver. And it wasn't exactly pillow talk.

She shook off the feeling of unease that rose inside her every time she thought about her looming conversation with Rhys and turned her attention back to his assistant, who was peeling the banana. "Is it safe to take the boat out?"

Collins shrugged. "The rain's stopped. Surf's a little choppy, but nothing I can't handle."

"Does that mean we can go to the beach now?" Oliver asked, snatching another cookie from the plate in front of him and shoving the whole thing into his mouth.

"Not if the surf is rough." Mallory tapped a finger against her chin, an idea forming. She eyed Collins. "How long are you planning on staying ashore?"

"Why?"

"There's a movie theater in Key West, isn't there?"

"No." He bit off the top of the banana.

"Is too," Oliver piped up, a spray of cookie crumbs following each word. "Mrs. Flannigan saw the last Avengers movie there. She likes Captain America best, like me. She brought me a poster and a box of Mike and Ikes."

"There is," Collins admitted. "But if you're asking me to take you there, the answer is no."

Mallory pulled the plate of cookies toward her, took one, and bit into it. Still warm. Chocolate chip, the Worthington Hotel's special, super-secret recipe. They gave one to all their guests when they checked in.

She licked a smear of melted chocolate from her lower lip and pinned Collins with her most intimidating stare. At least she hoped it was intimidating. Intimidation was so not her forte. Where was Brooke when she needed her? Probably off shagging her sexy new husband somewhere.

As if Mallory could complain. It wasn't like she hadn't been getting her fair share of shagging lately.

Focus. Stop thinking about Rhys's talented hands. Or his magic mouth. Or his...

"Why not?" she asked, stopping her thoughts in their naughty tracks and getting back to the matter at hand. "We're going a little stir-crazy. As beautiful as it is here, it would be nice to get off the island for a change."

Collins frowned and chewed his banana thoughtfully. "Mr. Dalton wouldn't approve."

"I'd like to hear that from him." She stood.

"He's on a conference call with the New York office," Collins explained. "He can't be interrupted."

"Then I'll leave him a note. It'll be fine." She polished off the cookie and wiped her hands on her jeans.

"I doubt that."

"I'll take full responsibility."

"That's what I'm afraid of."

"Please." Oliver looked up at them with wide, pleading eyes and a desperate, vulnerable look on his flushed face no doubt calculated for maximum pathetic effect. Kid was a fast learner. "I wanna go. I've never been to a movie theater."

"Never?" Mallory had to practically pick her jaw up off the floor. He must be exaggerating. What preschooler had never been to the movies?

Oliver shook his head, his blond bangs flopping on his forehead. "Nope."

This one, apparently. And she thought she'd been sheltered.

"That settles it." She pointed toward the door. "Go upstairs and get your raincoat. We're going to the movies."

He jumped out of his seat so fast his chair almost toppled over. "What are we going to see?"

"We'll use my phone to figure that out on the way over." They always had at least one G-rated movie playing, didn't they?

"Can we get popcorn with lots of butter?"

"You bet."

"And candy and soda?"

She tousled his hair. "The works."

With a gap-toothed grin as wide as if it were Christmas morning and he'd discovered a pile of presents beneath the tree, Oliver sprinted out of the kitchen.

Collins grimaced. "I've got a bad feeling about this."

"You worry too much." Mallory fished her wallet out of her purse and leafed through the bills inside. Twenty, forty, sixty, and a handful of ones and fives. More than enough for an afternoon at the movies. She dropped the wallet back into her pocketbook and scanned the counter for a pen and something to write on. She settled for one of the muffin-tin crayons and the back of an envelope. "Get the boat ready. We'll meet you at the dock in a few minutes."

"You're the boss." Collins tossed his banana peel in the trash can under the sink. "But don't say I didn't warn you."

Mallory scrawled a quick note to Rhys and stuck it on the refrigerator, figuring he was bound to get hungry and come searching for food at some point. Then she collected her purse and poncho, met Oliver at the bottom of the stairs, and together they headed to the dock.

Within minutes, they were safely in the back of the launch, zipping across the choppy, gray-green Atlantic with Collins at the helm. They huddled together against the wind as she called up the site for the movie theater on her cell phone browser, Oliver bouncing excitedly and chattering in her ear all the way.

"Sit still," she warned with a hand on his shoulder, her laugh taking away some of the sting of her words. "You'll never make it to the movies if you fall overboard and wind up as fish food."

"Fish food?" he asked, his eyes big as saucers. "You mean

if I fell in the fish would eat me?"

"No, silly." She'd forgotten how literal kids could be. "It's only an expression."

She pointed to a picture on her phone's screen, eager for a distraction. "How about this one? It has a talking robot and a time machine."

By the time they reached Key West, they'd agreed on the new Pixar film and arranged to meet Collins at the marina when the movie was over. She called for an Uber, and they made it to the theater in time to stock up on snacks at the concession stand and catch the last preview.

"That. Was. Awesome," Oliver exclaimed as the credits rolled ninety minutes later. "Can we come back and see it again tomorrow?"

"Not tomorrow." Mallory held up his rain slicker by the collar. "But sometime soon."

"Can Dad come too?" He poked his sticklike arms through the sleeves of his jacket. "He loves robots."

"I hope so." She felt a pang of guilt at not including Rhys in today's adventure. Not her choice, really. But still, he was Oliver's father. It would have been nice if he could have been there to see his son's face light up when the opening credits flashed bigger than life across the twenty-foot-tall screen. Maybe that was what Collins was talking about when he said Rhys wouldn't approve. Why hadn't she thought of that earlier?

No use beating herself up now. She'd explain it to Rhys when they returned home. Hopefully over dinner, if he could make time to join them. She'd asked Collins to pick up some fresh mahi-mahi she could grill and serve with her signature mango-lime salsa. That should tempt Rhys out of his cave.

She slipped her poncho over her head and bent to retrieve her purse from under her seat. "We'd better get moving. We don't want to keep Collins waiting."

The ride back to Flamingo Key was quiet. Oliver's eyelids started drooping the second his life jacket was fastened. Before they hit open water, his eyes had closed, and his head lolled against her shoulder. When they reached the island and the boat was secured, Mallory handed the still-sleeping Oliver over to Collins, who carried him to the house. She grabbed her purse and the insulated bag with the mahi-mahi and scrambled out after them, hurrying to catch up.

"Can you take him to his room?" she asked, keeping her voice low so she wouldn't wake Oliver as she opened the sliding glass door leading from the patio into the house. "He's exhausted. He can nap before dinner."

"Yes, Collins," Rhys drawled from an overstuffed chair in the corner. His words may have been directed at his assistant, but his eyes never left Mallory. The note she'd tacked to the refrigerator was crumpled in one hand, a drink in the other. "That's an excellent suggestion. Take Oliver to his room. Miss Worthington and I need to talk."

. . .

"What the hell were you thinking?" Rhys barked once his assistant and son had left the room. Mallory winced, and for a moment he regretted his outburst. Then he remembered the panic that had gripped him when he'd read the note clutched in his hand. He crushed it into a ball and threw it down onto the hardwood floor.

"Strike that." He rose, pacing from one side of the room to the other like a caged tiger. "You weren't thinking if for one second you thought I'd let you take Oliver off the island."

"Let me?" She dropped her bags on the floor behind the couch and folded her arms across her chest. "Last time I checked, entertaining your son was part of my job description. I didn't realize I needed your blessing for every item on our daily agenda."

"When it involves Oliver's safety, you do."

"His safety?" She gaped at him like he was speaking a foreign language. "We went to the movies. He never left my sight. And don't worry, it was rated G."

"You took him off the island," he repeated, stressing each word so there was no way she could fail to understand what had upset him.

If Mallory was gaping at him before, now she was gawking like a fish, her mouth opening and closing wordlessly. It took her a minute to speak. "Are you telling me Oliver's never left Flamingo Key?"

"Not since we came here after his mother died." Rhys stopped pacing and tossed back what remained of his scotch. His second—or was it third?—since discovering his son was missing. Okay, missing was an overstatement. More like AWOL. Which, in Rhys's opinion, was just as bad.

"And you?"

"Only when necessary."

Mallory shook her head incredulously. "He said he'd never been to the movies, but I didn't realize he was a prisoner here."

"He's not a prisoner." Rhys waved a hand at their surroundings. "Look around. This isn't exactly Sing Sing."

"A gilded cage is still a cage." Mallory's expression softened, an almost wistful look crossing her face. "It can't compare with freedom. And you can't keep him here forever."

"I know that. But he's only a child. It's my job to keep him safe."

He pinched the bridge of his nose and rolled his shoulders. Christ, this was exhausting. It didn't help that he'd been working day and night trying to lock down a contract with the Department of Defense. But if he sealed this deal, he could take it easy for a while. Spend more time with Oliver and Mallory. Family time, doing family things. Things he couldn't imagine taking pleasure in again before Mallory came along and shook up his world with her mealtime ultimatums and picnic abductions and late-night visits to the previously impenetrable fortress of his bedroom.

Rhys was so lost in thought he didn't notice she'd moved next to him until she laid a hand on his forearm, making him flinch. The hand tightened its grip, not letting him shake it off. When she spoke, her voice was gentle but firm. "Like you couldn't do for Beth?"

Her words, her touch, took some of the fight out of him. As usual, she'd seen right through him. It amazed him how this woman he'd known for a matter of months could read him so easily.

Yes, he'd wanted to punch walls when he read her note. But he didn't want to argue with her now. He wanted her to understand what he was doing and why.

He sank into the nearest seat, which turned out to be the sectional, and stared into his empty glass. "She wasn't supposed to be downtown that morning."

Mallory sat next to him, close but not touching, listening but not speaking.

"I left some paperwork at home," he continued, still staring at the bottom of his glass. "She was bringing it to me at the office."

Mallory turned toward him. "Life's strange that way."

"It was sheer dumb luck she didn't have Oliver with her. He had a cold, so she left him with a neighbor."

"None of that makes her death your fault."

"Doesn't it?" He slammed his glass down on the coffee table. "She wanted to leave New York. Begged me to move here full time. But I said no. Told her Argos needed me in the city. I put my damn job before my family."

"You did what you thought was right. You had no way of

knowing what was going to happen."

"I did what I thought was right for me. What was easiest for me." He shoved a hand through his already-disheveled hair. "I should have listened to her. She'd still be here if I had."

"Again, you don't know that. None of us know how much time we have on this planet. But that's no reason to hold Oliver hostage."

"You don't get it. I promised to protect him. I'm doing that the best way I know how."

"I get more than you think." Mallory cleared her throat and fiddled with her necklace. "There's something I need to tell you."

"Nothing good ever starts with those words." Rhys picked up his empty glass and went to the minibar for a refill. Whatever was coming next, he had a feeling it would go down better with a stiff drink.

She crossed and uncrossed her legs nervously. "I know how Oliver feels because I was like him growing up."

He stopped mid-pour. "Your mother died?"

"No." She shook her head. "But from the time I was twelve I felt like a prisoner in my own home."

"Why twelve?"

"That's when I was diagnosed with cancer."

Cancer. The word hit him like a sharp right hook to the gut, bringing back memories of his mother, her once-healthy frame thin and pale in a hospital bed.

"Non-Hodgkin lymphoma," she explained. "My parents reacted a lot like you. They thought the best way to make sure I got and stayed healthy was to keep me as close as possible. For a long time, I went along with it. I'd caused them enough pain. Why make them worry any more than they already did? Then one day I woke up and realized the life I was living wasn't my own. So I left. And came here. I guess the rest is history."

Her eyes met his, the uncertainty in them another punch to his midsection. "I've wanted to tell you for a while, but I didn't know how you'd react. "

"Are you—? Is it—?"

He couldn't complete the thought, but she understood and answered anyway.

"I've been in remission for years, but I get follow-up care every six months. There's always the risk it will come back, or I'll develop another kind of cancer."

He set down the bottle and downed what little he'd managed to get into his glass before her shocking revelation. Shocking, but the more he thought about it not surprising. Her veiled comment about survivor's guilt made complete sense now. How many of her fellow patients had she watched lose their battles with cancer? "I don't know what to say."

"Say you won't put Oliver through what I went through. Say you won't suffocate him. Say you'll let him be a regular kid."

"He is a regular kid."

"Regular kids go to the movies. And playgrounds, parties, and playdates. They socialize with other kids." Mallory's voice rose with each new example. "Please. Don't do to him what my parents did to me. It took me years to work up enough courage to break free. I won't live like that again, and I won't stand by and watch Oliver live that way, either. I care for him—and you—too much to let that happen."

Rhys ditched the glass and returned to the sofa. More alcohol wasn't going to solve this problem.

"I know I'll have to lighten up eventually." His stomach knotted at the admission. "But I feel like I'm making real progress with him. I can't let him go now."

"You're not letting him go," Mallory insisted. "You're letting him live."

"I can't. Not yet." Rhys rested his elbows on his knees and buried his head in his hands.

"If not now, then when?"

"I don't know," he answered honestly, his voice muffled by his hands. "I'm sorry. I wish I could give you a better answer."

Silence hung heavy in the air between them for a long moment.

"I'm sorry, too," she said finally, her voice catching on the last word.

He lifted his head. His insides twisted at the tears swimming in her eyes. "What are you saying?"

She looked down at her lap. "I'm saying there's only one thing left for me to do."

"What's that?"

His heart stopped in his chest as he waited an agonizing minute that seemed like hours for her response. When she raised her head, the tears that had been brimming in her eyes spilled down her beautiful, serene face.

"Pack."

Chapter Fourteen

"Thanks for letting me crash with you guys. I promise I won't stay long."

Mallory dropped her weekender tote at the foot of the bed in the larger of her sister's two spare bedrooms. Funny, she thought, staring at the familiar bag. She'd left Florida the same way she'd come. Just the one piece of luggage, the rest of her belongings on a truck somewhere along the I-95 corridor.

No. That wasn't entirely true. She'd left with a lot more baggage than she brought. She just carried it on the inside.

"Stay as long as you like," Brooke said, crossing to the window and opening the blinds to let in some late-afternoon sunlight. "We've got plenty of room. And Brooklyn's way more hip than Huntington."

"Anywhere Mom and Dad aren't is more hip." Mallory shuddered at the thought of moving back to her parents' Long Island estate. She owed her sister big-time for sparing her from that humiliation. Which was why overstaying her welcome wasn't an option. "But I don't want to cramp your newlywed style."

"More like you don't want to listen to us go at it all night long," Brooke teased.

"Please." Mallory sat on the bed. "That's an image I can't unsee."

"Don't worry." Brooke plopped down next to her. "You won't hear a thing. The walls in this place are really thick. Eli designed them to keep the heat in in the winter and out in the summer. The soundproofing's an added bonus."

"The next thing I know you'll be telling me you have a red room of pain."

"No." Brooke kicked off her Chuck Taylors and tucked her feet underneath her. "We thought about it but opted for a wine cellar instead."

"On the fifth floor? Very funny."

Mallory flopped onto her back, fighting a yawn. Travel always wore her out, and today was no exception. Long lines at TSA. Packed plane. Getting stuck between two guys who could have been sumo wrestlers with an antsy toddler behind her, kicking her seat back for the entire three-hour flight home.

Strike that. Not home. Home was Flamingo Key. Or had been. Now she was drifting, like a ship without a port, until she got her next assignment from the staffing agency. Which, according to Alison, wouldn't be long. No kids this time, just cooking, per Mallory's request.

If leaving Rhys had been heartbreaking, leaving Oliver was gut-wrenching. No amount of explaining could convince him that even though it was time for her to move on, she still cared for him. All he could see was that another woman he'd grown to love and depend on was deserting him. By the time she stepped onto the launch with Collins for her final ride, they'd both shed enough tears to flood the Atlantic Ocean.

It was an experience she had zero desire to repeat.

Mallory covered her eyes with one arm and tried to

regulate her breathing. In, out. Slow and steady. Her own version of playing possum. Maybe if she lay there like that long enough her sister would get the hint and give her some peace and quiet before starting the inevitable interrogation.

"So…" Brooke let the word dangle, and Mallory's stomach churned with the knowledge she wasn't going to like what was coming next. So much for her sister getting the hint. "Are you going to tell me what happened with von Dreamy? Last I heard you two were hot and heavy."

"It's complicated."

"It usually is, especially when sex is involved. Of course…" Brooke paused for dramatic effect. "If it was more than sex, then it's even more complicated."

Mallory opted for the safest course and stayed silent, knowing she'd give herself away if she spoke. It was more than sex for her and, she was almost certain, for Rhys. They'd never said the words, but the feeling was there in every kiss, every touch, every secret, shared smile.

She loved Rhys Dalton. She loved his razor-sharp mind, his huge heart, how he could make her laugh one second and moan with pleasure the next. She especially loved the way he made her feel—cherished and important and more alive than ever before.

But what good was loving him when she couldn't be with him, not if it meant being an accomplice in isolating his son? She hadn't come this far—bucking her parents' wishes, quitting her job, leaving New York—only to take a giant step backward by going against everything her hard-fought independence stood for.

It was true what they said about standing on principle. More often than not, it meant standing alone.

"Was it?" Brooke prodded.

"Was it what?" Mallory asked, not ready to say out loud what her heart was silently screaming.

Brooke let out a frustrated huff. "More than sex."

"I haven't unpacked. Do we have to do this now?" Mallory sat up. Feigning sleep was a bust. Once her sister got started, she was relentless, like a hungry dog with a particularly juicy bone. "I've seen *Law & Order*. Even criminals get a glass of water and a cigarette before the cops start questioning them."

"You don't smoke."

"You know what I mean."

"Trust me, you'll feel better getting it off your chest." Brooke put her arm around Mallory and gave her a quick squeeze. "And who knows? I might be able to help. Remember what a hot mess I was when I found out Eli had lied about his job and hidden that he was buying this building?"

"Hot mess is putting it lightly. You were drowning yourself in junk food and diet soda."

"That's not the point. The point is you talked me off the ledge and convinced me to listen to him."

"That was different."

"How?"

"I was the one giving the advice. I'm the sensible, look-before-you-leap one. You're Miss Close-Your-Eyes-and-Jump-Without-a-Net."

Mallory swung her legs over the side of the bed and stood, stretching her arms over her head. Her back creaked in protest, making her wince. It was going to take hot yoga or a deep tissue massage—or both—for her body to recuperate from three hours of being in the middle of a sumo sandwich.

But at least her body had a shot at recovery. She wasn't sure her heart would ever mend.

Brooke lifted a shoulder and let it fall in a careless shrug. "That might be true. But I'm the one with a smoking-hot husband who lives to give me orgasms, and you're spending the foreseeable future sleeping alone in our guest room."

"Ouch."

"I'm sorry. That came out wrong."

"You don't say?" Mallory arched a brow at her sister, who responded by rolling her eyes. "I rest my case about which one of us is the better advice-giver."

"What I meant was sometimes leaping without looking isn't so bad. As long as there's someone there to catch you."

"Catch, yes. Trap, no."

"Explain."

"First I need sustenance. Please tell me you have something in your cupboard besides potato chips and Ho Hos."

"Sure." Brooke sprang off the bed, her stockinged feet making a soft *thud* on the polished oak floor. "I've also got an unopened package of powdered mini doughnuts, half a bag of Cool Ranch Doritos, and some Ben & Jerry's Cherry Garcia."

"I see marriage to a multimillionaire hasn't given you a taste for haute cuisine."

"Billionaire," her sister corrected. "And if you asked me, there's no finer dining than a handful of Cheetos, a pack of Slim Jims, and a couple of Twinkies, with a Diet Coke chaser."

Mallory followed Brooke to the kitchen. She pulled up a stool at the massive center island while her sister managed to rustle up a not-entirely-unhealthy assortment of cheese, crackers, and a few sad-looking grapes. Mallory thought of the omelet she prepared the night Rhys first kissed her. Or their food foreplay after they rescued Oliver.

She stared at the pathetic plate in front of her. Oh, how the lovelorn had fallen.

"Okay." Brooke took the stool across from Mallory and propped her chin on her hands. "Enough stalling. I fed you. Let's hear all the dirty details."

Mallory took a chance on a sad grape—bad idea, she thought, grimacing at the sour squirt as she bit into it—and launched into the whole saga of her trip to the movie theater with Oliver and Rhys's reaction.

"That's it?" Brooke pulled the plate toward herself and sandwiched a piece of cheese between two crackers. "You bailed because he got mad at you for taking his kid to the movies without asking first?"

"No, that's not it." Mallory snatched the plate back. "I bailed—your word, not mine—because I wasn't about to stick around and do nothing while Rhys kept Oliver under house arrest."

"Don't you think you're overreacting a teeny-tiny bit?" Brooke asked through a mouthful of cheese and cracker.

"You wouldn't understand. You weren't the one under lock and key. Mom and Dad let you do whatever you wanted, wherever you wanted, with whoever you wanted. While I had to fight tooth and nail to go to school three hours away, and they only let me do that after I promised to come home after graduation and work at the Worthington."

"Fine." Brooke reached down and pulled two cans of soda from the under-counter beverage refrigerator. She popped the top on one and slid the other across to Mallory. "For the sake of argument, I'll concede your reaction was totally normal, given the circumstances. But who says you have to do nothing?"

"Rhys." Mallory opened her soda and drank. "I tried reasoning with him. He wouldn't listen."

"How hard did you try?"

"What are you getting at?"

"Think of it from his point of view." Brooke took a sip from her can and wiped her mouth with the back of her hand. "He lost his wife. Blames himself. Doesn't want to go through that again with his son."

Mallory sighed. "I'm not unsympathetic. But Mom and Dad's motives were noble, too. They were trying to protect me. But that doesn't make what they did right."

"From what you told me, Rhys isn't Mom and Dad. He admitted he'd have to cut the cord at some point. Our parents would have been happy to keep you in lockdown in perpetuity if you hadn't grown a pair and flown the nest."

"True," Mallory admitted after thinking about it for a minute. "But…"

"And you could make sure he stuck to his word and started to let Oliver do more regular kid stuff. Like Maria sewed the von Trapp kids clothes out of curtains, so they could climb trees and row boats and play leapfrog."

"How many times do I have to tell you? This isn't *The Sound of Music*. This is my life."

Brooke plucked another slice of cheese from the plate between them and bit off one corner. "You know it's based on a true story, right?"

"'Based on' being the operative words. It's highly fictionalized."

"You're missing the point."

"Which is what?" Mallory gave her sister her best evil-eyed glare. She didn't know what Brooke expected her to do. Hypnotize Rhys into submission? Use her limited powers of sexual persuasion? That was sure to be a bust. She was no femme fatale by any stretch of the imagination. "I told you, I tried…"

"Try harder." Brooke accepted Mallory's challenge, meeting her stare. It wasn't in her sister's nature to back down, a quality Mallory usually admired but at the moment wished was a little less predominant. "If Rhys Dalton is worth it—if his son's worth it—you owe it to them both to try harder."

"How?"

"Baby steps, little sis. Baby steps. The man's been a virtual hermit for three years. You can't expect him to change overnight."

"Even if we could reach some sort of understanding about Oliver, there's my cancer to think about."

"What cancer?" Brooke scoffed. "You don't have cancer. You've been in remission for over ten years."

"There's always a chance of a recurrence or a secondary cancer."

"How does Rhys feel about it?" Brooke leaned in, resting her elbows on the counter. "You did tell him, didn't you?"

Mallory nodded.

"How did he react?"

"We didn't have much of a chance to discuss it. We were focused on Oliver. But his mother died from cancer, so…"

Brooke jabbed a finger across the counter at Mallory's chest. "So you haven't got any idea if it's a deal breaker or not."

"I can't imagine he's eager to jump into a long-term relationship with someone who's got an expiration date."

"We all have an expiration date, Mal. None of us come with a warranty." The accusatory finger lowered, and Brooke covered Mallory's hand with hers. "Keep looking for excuses, and you're going to find them. Or you could look for solutions, and you might be surprised."

"Anybody home?" The front lock clicked open and Eli's voice bounced off the walls of the huge high-ceilinged apartment.

Brooke's face lit up and she leaped off her stool. "In the kitchen, babe."

Eli appeared a few seconds later in the doorway, a bag with what looked like the logo of a Chinese restaurant in one hand and a stack of mail in the other.

"Hey, sweetheart. Mallory." He deposited both bag and mail on the counter before giving his sister-in-law a quick hug and his wife a long, lingering, almost embarrassing kiss. "I hope you're in the mood for something spicy. I brought takeout from Szechuan Gourmet."

"Sounds great. I'm starving." Brooke's stomach grumbled as if to emphasize her point. Her husband laughed and started unpacking the bags.

"Looks like we got a few more RSVPs," he said, gesturing toward the pile of envelopes and catalogs.

"Oh, goody." Brooke's sarcastic tone and exaggerated eye roll said it was anything but good. "I'll open them later. Probably more of Mom's country club cronies. Why did I let her convince me to go through with this ridiculous reception? I swear, I'm not going to know a single person at this shindig."

"You'll know me." Eli came up behind his wife, wrapped his arms around her, and dropped a kiss to the nape of her neck.

"And me." Mallory stood. "I need to change out of my travel clothes. I'll be back in a few minutes. Feel free to start dinner without me."

With a pasted-on smile and what she hoped was a suitably jaunty wave, she turned to leave. She needed a few minutes of solitude. A time-out from her sister's newly wedded bliss. As happy as she was for Brooke, watching her with Eli was a special kind of torture. Like a thousand knives to her fragile heart.

"Hey," Brooke called after her.

Mallory stopped and spun around to face her sister, who was taking a stack of plates from one of the cabinets. "Yeah?"

Brooke handed the plates to Eli and pinned her sister with a worried frown. "You okay?"

Mallory brushed off her sister's concern with another wave and started back toward her temporary bedroom.

"I'm fine," she said over her shoulder. "Just tired. And hungry. I'll feel better when I have some of that Szechuan."

And when she figured out what to do about her train wreck of a life.

Brooke's last words before Eli interrupted their conversation echoed in her head. Was she going to keep making excuses not to be with Rhys?

Or was her sister right, and it was time to start looking for solutions?

• • •

The sun had sunk well below the horizon and stars dotted the cloudless night sky when Rhys emerged from his office, his usually neat hair unruly and two—or was it three?—days' growth on his chin.

He made his way across the foyer, through the great room, and into the kitchen, the only sounds the squeak of his shoes on the tile floor and the low hum of the air-conditioning. Had his house always been this big? Or did it just seem that way now that Mallory wasn't there, filling the empty spaces with smiles and laughter and fancy food? Empty spaces he hadn't realized existed until she showed up on his doorstep, as unexpected and unpredictable as a sudden summer storm.

And she'd left the same way.

Rhys headed for the stairs to check on Oliver before trying to force himself to sleep at least a few hours. One thing that hadn't changed in Mallory's absence was his renewed commitment to his son. He hadn't hired a new nanny, and he was starting to think they didn't need one. Mrs. Flannigan swore she could handle the cooking, as long as they didn't expect anything close to Mallory's level. And if he cut back a bit, delegated more work to Collins and the staff in New York, put in most of his office hours after Oliver was in bed, they should be able to manage on their own.

Mallory would approve. So would Beth.

Maybe that was why he'd rejected every candidate the agency had submitted. One was too inexperienced, one too high-strung, another too gruff. Collins had started calling him Goldilocks under his breath, complaining he'd never find one who was just right.

Trouble was, he already had.

Rhys reached Oliver's bedroom and cracked the door open, expecting to find the room dark and his son sprawled across his bed, one pajama-clad leg sticking out from under the covers. Instead, the light was on and Oliver sat at the tiny table in the center of his room, a sheet of paper in front of him and a crayon clutched in one fist.

"Shouldn't you be asleep?" Rhys asked, squeezing himself into a pint-sized chair across from his son.

"I have to finish this first," Oliver said without looking up, his bangs flopping over his furrowed forehead as he scribbled furiously.

"Finish what?"

Oliver's crayon stilled, and he peered up at Rhys through the blond wisps of his bangs. "Promise you won't be mad."

Rhys frowned. "Why would I be mad?"

"It's a picture. For Mallory." Oliver's lower lip trembled. "To make her come back."

Rhys thought his heart couldn't rip apart any more than it already had. He was wrong. He swallowed the lump in his throat and gave his son a shaky smile. "Can I see?"

"Sure." Oliver pushed the paper across the table.

Rhys examined it for a few moments.

"Is this me?" he asked, pointing to the tallest of three stick figures.

"Uh-huh."

"Then this one must be you." He pointed to the smallest figure.

"Uh-huh." Oliver jabbed a finger proudly at the third figure. "And this is Mallory."

"I thought so." Rhys squinted at the drawing, his once-shaky smile threatening to break free and split his face. His son had many talents, but Vincent van Gogh he wasn't. Picasso, maybe, if the abstract nature of his drawing was anything to go by. "So, um, what are we doing in this picture?"

"Can't you tell?"

"Sure," Rhys lied. "But I want you to explain it to me."

"This is the Emperor State Building." Oliver pointed to a bright pink squiggle in one corner. His finger moved lower to a green blob. "And this is Center Park. They're in New York City. That's where Mallory's from. She told me. And Mrs. Flannigan said I used to live there, too."

"Yes, you did." Rhys absently traced the squiggle, his stomach knotting. Manhattan. Light years away from Flamingo Key, in distance and every other way imaginable. And the one island he'd hoped never to set foot on again. "So we're in New York?"

"Uh-huh."

"Why?"

"To say sorry."

Rhys looked up from the drawing to study his son. "You think I should apologize to Mallory?"

"Not you, me," Oliver said, his voice and expression deadpan, making him seem more solemn than any four-year-old had a right—or a reason—to be. "For getting her in trouble."

Rhys moved his chair closer to his son. "How did you get her in trouble?"

"I was bored." Oliver stared down at the table, his words spilling out in a jumbled rush. "Collins told her you wouldn't like it if she took me to the movies. But I'd never gone before, and I wanted to go really, really bad. So we went. And you got mad at her, and she left."

"Who said I was mad?" Rhys put an arm around his son's shoulders.

"Collins." Oliver pulled the picture back, picked up a yellow crayon, and started coloring again, probably adding some other New York City landmark to his already crowded drawing, like the Statue of Liberty or Times Square. "I heard him talking to Mrs. Flannigan. He said you were mad at Mallory for taking me off the island, and you used it as a 'cuse to chase her away because you were scared of her."

Not scared of her, Rhys thought, rubbing his neck, the two—or was it three?—days of stubble scraping his palm. Scared of his feelings for her.

Was Collins right? Was that what he'd done? Pushed Mallory away not only because he was afraid of losing Oliver, but because he was afraid of losing her, too?

"But you don't have to be scared of her," Oliver continued, scribbling away. His leaned forward and wrinkled his nose, all the four-year-old focus he could muster on the piece of paper in front of him. "She's nice. She always let me have the last piece of pizza and she smelled like ice cream and strawberries."

"Ice cream, huh?" Rhys chuckled. "What kind?"

Oliver put down his crayon. "Mint chocolate chip."

"Your favorite." Rhys squeezed his son's shoulder. "I'm not scared of Mallory, pal. And I'm not mad at her. Or you."

"Then why did she have to go away?"

Good question.

"It's a grown-up thing," Rhys said, taking the easy way out and ducking the issue. "I'll explain it to you when you're older."

Oliver puckered his lips and blew out a raspberry. "I hate grown-up things."

He switched to a purple crayon and went back to coloring.

"So do I sometimes," Rhys admitted.

Like this time.

He'd been an idiot. Let fear run his life. It had almost

cost him his relationship with Oliver. Would have, if Mallory hadn't come along to shake things up. And now it had cost him her.

He should have taken more time to listen to her, to try to understand where she was coming from. Why had he been so quick to dismiss her concerns? Valid concerns based on her own painful history.

Cancer. He couldn't even begin to imagine how hard it must have been for her to go through that as a teenager. It had been rough on his mother, and she was an adult. Mallory wasn't just bright and beautiful. She was brave, too.

He'd be lying if he said the thought of loving someone with Mallory's medical track record didn't scare the shit out of him. But he was more frightened by the prospect of not having her in his life at all than he was of losing her.

Rhys looked over at his son, still wrapped up in his artwork. The kid was right. Someone needed to apologize to Mallory. But it wasn't Oliver.

"All done." Oliver held up his drawing.

"Great job, buddy." Rhys took it from him and placed it safely in the center of the table. Then he picked up his son and stood. "Now back to bed."

"Can we send it to Mallory in the morning?" Oliver asked, winding his arms around Rhys's neck and pressing his face into his chest.

"I've got a better idea." Rhys laid his son down on the bed and pulled the covers up to his chin. Drastic times called for even more drastic measures, and there was only one way he could think of to make Mallory listen to him after how he'd treated her.

"Why don't we give it to her in person?"

Chapter Fifteen

Mallory had to hand it to her mother. She sure knew how to throw a party.

From her position behind a potted plant in the corner of the grand ballroom at the Worthington, Mallory sipped champagne as the cream of New York society ate, drank, and mingled. Waitstaff in crisp white shirts, black bow ties, and neatly pressed black pants circulated with trays of deviled quail eggs, bite-size bruschetta, and Veuve Clicquot.

At the center of it all stood Brooke and Eli, looking sleek and stylish in an off-white stretch jumpsuit and impeccably tailored charcoal-gray suit. Her sister shifted from one Louboutin-clad foot to the other, clearly uncomfortable with either the spike heels or all the attention being showered on her as the fairer half of the main attraction. Or both.

Eli slipped an arm around Brooke's waist and bent low to whisper something in her ear. Brooke threw her head back and laughed, then took her husband's face in her hands and kissed him, long and deep, both of them oblivious to or uncaring of the stuffed shirts looking on with shock and disapproval.

Mallory sank into the nearest chair with a sigh and drained the rest of her champagne. Would she ever love and be loved like that, so thoroughly the outside world ceased to matter? Was that what she'd given up by leaving Flamingo Key?

"Hiding again?" Her mother's censure was like a bucket of ice water splashed in her face.

"Not hiding, resting," Mallory corrected, although there was a bit of truth to both. Yes, she was trying to keep a low profile. But she was also dead tired. The past few days had been a flurry of activity leading up to the reception. Fittings. Florists. Favors. No detail was too small to go unattended to by Pamela Worthington and her army of minions, including her youngest daughter. "Besides, it's Brooke's big day, not mine."

"Well, I need you to come out of exile and come with me," her mother snapped. One hand fluttered to her throat, fingering the strand of pearls nestled there. "The Livingstons are here, and they've brought their son, Bryce. He's an attorney. Highly respected. Intellectual property, I think. I told him all about you, and he wants to meet you."

Her mother was practically salivating at this last bit of news. With her eldest daughter successfully married off, she'd shifted all of the focus of her matchmaking efforts to the sole remaining target.

Mallory.

Mallory signaled a passing waiter and exchanged her empty glass for a full one. She took a generous sip of sparkling liquid before speaking.

"I'm not really in the market for a boyfriend right now." Especially one handpicked by her mother. Been there, done that, not doing it again, whether or not Rhys was still in the picture. And given the radio silence she'd gotten from him since she left Flamingo Key, she was guessing the answer was not.

"But I promised his parents I'd introduce you two," her mother fumed. Was it too much to ask her to be happy—or at least pleasant—for one day? "They want him to settle down with a nice girl. And that horrible Vivian Richmond is here. If we don't move fast, she'll get to him first."

"Leave her alone, Pam." Mallory's father came up behind his wife, who bristled at the shortening of her name. "Can't you see she's not interested?"

"But…"

"The photographer is looking for you," he cut in. "Something about not having the right lens."

"Can't anyone do their job without my help?" her mother huffed as she stormed away. "I'm surrounded by incompetents."

Mallory stared after her. "I feel sorry for that photographer."

"Don't." Her father pulled up a chair next to her and sat. "I made it up."

"You what?"

"Made it up. He's got all the equipment he needs, which your mother will find out in about thirty seconds."

"Why lie?"

"To get your matchmaking mother off your back," he answered with a conspiratorial wink, crossing an ankle over his knee.

"I don't understand." Mallory gulped her champagne. She definitely needed more alcohol in her system for this surreal conversation. On the plus side, at least her father was talking to her again, even if it seemed like aliens had taken over his brain. "Mom has this bright idea if I start dating someone in New York I won't want to leave again. I thought you'd want that as much as she does."

"I want you near, of course." Her normally fastidious father loosened his tie and unbuttoned the first button of his dress shirt. The aliens at work again, she supposed. "But not if it means dating one of your mother's hand-selected stooges."

If she weren't already sitting, she would have collapsed from shock. Her parents always presented a united front. Her father's jumping ship was like a Blue Angel fighter pilot breaking formation. Unheard of. "Are you sure you're my father and not his doppelgänger?"

"Maybe I'm getting soft in my old age," he joked.

Her father. Joking. She looked around for the cameras, certain she was being punked. "The hard-ass of the hospitality industry? Soft isn't in your vocabulary."

His eyes shifted, and she followed his gaze to the dance floor, where Brooke and Eli swayed together as one, lost in each other. "Or maybe watching one daughter fall in love has made me want the same for the other."

Mallory stared into her glass, pretending to be fascinated by the bubbles in her champagne. It was too much to take in all at once. Brooke and Eli. Her father's abrupt attitude adjustment. Her feelings for Rhys. "I'm not sure that's in the cards for me."

"I won't ask what happened in Florida." She started to protest, but her father held up his hand. "Don't bother denying it. You haven't been the same since you came home."

He stiffened suddenly, his face blanching. "You're not sick again, are you?"

"I'm fine, Dad." She put a hand over his and squeezed. "My last checkup was cancer-free."

"Thank God." His whole posture relaxed, and some of the color returned to his cheeks. He leaned back in his chair and fixed her with a look of deep concern she'd experienced countless times throughout her childhood, usually from a hospital bed. "I want you to know there will always be a place for you here at the Worthington."

She squeezed his hand again. "I know, Dad. And that means a lot to me."

Not that she was going back there any time soon. She'd already had several offers from the staffing agency, and she was weighing her options. She was even considering opening her own business. Maybe something with kids in the kitchen. Oliver had loved it when they'd cooked together. Whatever she wound up doing, she wasn't about to give up her newfound independence, not after what it had cost her.

Her heart.

"But if you've got unfinished business with this Dalton fellow…" Her father let the sentence hang.

Mallory almost choked on her champagne. "Why would I have unfinished business with Rhys?"

Her father arched an aristocratic brow. "On a first-name basis, are you?"

She blushed and drained her drink.

"Heaven knows I'm not one to give advice to the lovelorn," he went on, risking a glance at her mother, who had finished with the poor photographer and moved on to some hapless waiter, wagging a finger in his face, no doubt berating him for some minor transgression.

Mallory wondered not for the first time what her parents saw in each other. They acted more like business partners or not-so-polite strangers than lovers. With an example like that, it was a miracle either one of their daughters was in a healthy, committed relationship.

She supposed it was too much to hope for lightning to strike twice.

"I'm not lovelorn," she lied, wishing her glass weren't empty. Her eyes flickered around the room, trying to catch the one of the waitstaff. Instead, they landed on a familiar three-and-a-half-foot towhead. She blinked and shook her head to clear it, certain her mind was playing tricks on her.

Nope. There he was, as real as the cake she'd spent half the night decorating, running toward her and calling her name.

She jumped up, almost tipping over her chair. "Oliver?"

"Mallory." The little boy launched himself at her, wrapping his arms around her legs.

Her father rose beside her and cleared his throat. "Who is this young man?"

"I'm Oliver Trent Dalton." He released Mallory and stuck out a hand to her father, looking like a heartbreaking miniature of his father in a navy-blue polo shirt, perfectly creased khakis, and shiny cordovan loafers.

"Dalton, eh?" Her father took the boy's eager hand in his and shook it, shooting a questioning sideways glance at Mallory. "Pleasure to meet you."

"Really, Mallory." Her mother reappeared, lips pursed, her ire transferred from the hapless waiter to her youngest daughter. She glared at Mallory, then at Oliver, then back at Mallory again. "The invitation clearly said adults only."

Mallory ignored her, kneeling so she was eye level with Oliver. Her heartbeat thudded in her ears, and she wiped her suddenly damp palms on her skirt. Questions spilled from her trembling lips like chocolate from the four-tiered fountain in the center of the room. "What are you doing here? How did you get to New York? Where's your father?"

"He's right here."

That voice. Deep, rich, and utterly male. It never failed to send a thrill quivering through her body, and this time was no exception.

She dragged her eyes upward to see Rhys, dressed almost identically to his son, hands in the pockets of his khakis. His handsome face looked haggard, as if he hadn't been sleeping any better than she had since she left Flamingo Key. But his whiskey eyes were as sharp and clear as always. They locked on hers, sucking the air out of her.

"And he's not leaving until you hear what he came to say."

• • •

This was not how Rhys had envisioned this moment.

It should have been easy. Fly to New York. Go to the address on Mallory's employment paperwork. Beg, plead, and grovel, not necessarily in that order. Repeat as often as necessary until she forgave him.

Instead, he and Oliver had gone on a wild-goose chase from Long Island to Brooklyn to Manhattan, finally tracking Mallory down at the hotel that bore her family name.

Yet another surprise. His Mallory was a hotel heiress.

If she was still his Mallory.

He pulled at his shirt collar, not sure where to begin. The unfamiliar uncertainty clawed at his gut. In business, he was used to being in charge, having all the answers. But he was seriously out of practice in the romance department.

The growing audience wasn't helping matters, either. From the trays of canapés and cocktails, the fancy table linens, and the well-dressed attendees, it was obvious he'd interrupted some sort of celebration. The music had stopped, and the crowd was becoming aware of the drama playing out in the corner.

"Dad," Oliver prompted in a stage whisper, tugging at Rhys's pant leg. "You're supposed to 'pologize, remember? So Mallory will come back home with us. And don't forget to give her the picture I drew."

"This is a private function," a woman who looked like she'd been sucking on lemons said with a sniff, one designer shoe tapping impatiently on the plush carpet. "You'll have to leave."

Mallory's mother, he assumed. And he'd already annoyed her. He was off to a great start.

"I'm sorry." *Not.* But he tried his best to look contrite. "I need to speak with Mallory. It's important."

"What's going on?" A stunning brunette in a white jumpsuit joined their not-so-merry band, accompanied by a tall, equally dark-haired man with a possessive arm around her waist.

"Your sister seems to think this is a block party," Mallory's mother huffed. "She's invited half the neighborhood."

"Two people are hardly half the neighborhood. And I didn't invite them. They just showed up. All the way from Florida. Without so much as a word of warning." Mallory turned to him with wide, questioning eyes. "Phones not working on the island? Internet down?"

Rhys shuffled his feet. "I thought it would be more dramatic this way."

"We wanted to surprise you," Oliver chimed in, hopping up and down. "Did we?"

"You sure did," Mallory said, smiling down at him warmly. The invisible band constricting Rhys's heart loosened. She couldn't be too mad at him if she could look at his son like that, right? "Color me surprised."

"Oh. My. God." The brunette—Mallory's sister, Rhys figured—eyed him like she was sizing up a cut of prime rib at a butcher shop and squealed. Actually squealed, so loud he was surprised glass didn't break. "You're von Dreamy."

Rhys frowned. "Von who?"

"Don't mind Brooke." Mallory shot her sister a glare that could have melted steel. "She doesn't know what she's saying when she's off her meds. None of us do."

"Dad." Oliver tugged at his pants leg again. "The 'pology. Quick. Before the mean lady makes us leave."

"Don't worry, young man. No one's going to make you

leave." A distinguished-looking older man in a tuxedo, who Rhys had deduced was Mallory's father, took her mother by the elbow. "Come on, Pam. Let's give Mallory and her friends some privacy."

"If they wanted privacy, they wouldn't be having this conversation in the middle of a wedding reception, would they?" The toe-tapping stopped. In its place, Mallory's mother tented her fingers, drumming them together to demonstrate her continued irritation.

"Good idea." Rhys gestured toward the door. "Why don't we take this into the hall?"

"It's Oliver, right?" Brooke asked, addressing his son. "How would you like to try out the chocolate fountain with me?"

Oliver's eyes lit up. "You have a chocolate fountain?"

"Sure do," the man with her answered. "With all kinds of fruit for dipping. Plus, a whole bunch of stuff that's bad for you, like sponge cake, Rice Krispies Treats, and marshmallows."

"Marshmallows?" Oliver licked his lips. "I love marshmallows."

"Those were my idea." Brooke gave her mother an I-told-you-so look.

Oliver looked to Rhys for approval. "Can I, Dad?"

Rhys nodded. "You bet."

"And you'll give Mallory my drawing?"

Rhys patted his chest, where Oliver's picture was tucked safely away in the inside pocket of his jacket. "It's right here."

Mallory's eyes darted from him to Oliver, then back again. "You're okay with Brooke watching him?"

"She's your sister, right?"

"Yeah, but I thought…"

"You thought wrong." Rhys ruffled his son's hair and gave him a pat on the back, nudging him toward Mallory's sister. "Have fun, buddy. And be good. Pay attention to

Brooke. We'll be back soon."

"Okay. And Dad?"

"Yeah?"

"Try not to mess up the 'pology."

Rhys chuckled. "I'll do my best."

"Don't worry about us." Brooke put an arm around Oliver. "We'll be fine. By the time you two have patched things up, we'll be riding a sugar high."

"You don't have to do this," Mallory protested. Rhys made a mental note of the fact that she didn't contradict her sister's assumption they'd be able to patch things up. The band around his heart loosened a bit more. "It's your wedding reception."

"Are you kidding?" Brooke squeezed Oliver's shoulder. "I'd rather hang with this little dude than most of the people on the guest list."

Mallory's mother cleared her throat accusingly.

"Fine. Half then," Brooke amended, leading Oliver across the room, her husband at her elbow. "All right, men. Forward march. That chocolate's not going to eat itself."

Rhys motioned with his head to the door. "Shall we?"

Mallory's mother started to object, but her father cut her off with a raised hand. "Go. We'll hold down the fort here."

"Thanks, Dad." Mallory gave her father a grateful smile and turned to Rhys. "Come on. I know somewhere we won't be disturbed."

"Good." Rhys followed her out of the ballroom and into the hotel lobby.

"Where are we going?" he asked.

"Upstairs. My mother rented a suite for the wedding party." She stopped in front of a bank of elevators and punched the up button. "I'm not doing this in the hallway. Too many prying eyes."

They rode the short distance to the third floor in silence.

Once there, she led him a few feet down the hall, stopped in front of one of the rooms, and pulled a plastic key card from a cleverly hidden pocket in her fancy dress.

He took a minute to drink in his fill of her as she fumbled with the key card. Her blue-green dress was simple but stunning, hugging her curves like a jealous lover until it ended above the knee, leaving her smooth, shapely legs bare to the straps of her spiky heels. She was everything he wanted, everything he needed, and more. Smart. Sensitive. Strong. And adorably nervous as she struggled with the key.

He swallowed. Hard. Oliver was right. He'd better not mess this up.

After a few tries, she unlocked the door and ushered him inside. She went straight for the minibar, grabbing two bottles of wine and holding them aloft, what looked like a malbec in her right hand and a chardonnay in her left. "Red or white?"

He shook his head. He needed to be totally lucid for this conversation. Anything less increased the fuckup factor exponentially. "I'm fine, thanks."

"White it is." She screwed the top off, removed the frilly paper covers from two hotel tumblers, and poured.

He took the glass she handed him but set it down on a side table without drinking. "Thanks for agreeing to hear me out."

Way to start strong, Romeo. Maybe he should have that drink after all. His game couldn't get much worse.

"It's the least I can do. You came all this way. Left Flamingo Key. Brought Oliver with you. After everything you said..." Mallory sipped her chardonnay. Even across the room, Rhys could see her pulse beat at the hollow of her throat. The rapid, irregular rhythm matched his. "I don't understand."

"It's called a grand gesture." He stepped closer. "When a guy puts himself out there to show a girl how he feels."

Her breath hitched, and she ran a finger around the rim of her glass. "And how do you feel?"

"Like an idiot for not listening to you." He took another step, his obvious effect on her making him bolder. "You were right about Oliver. About everything."

The mention of his son's name reminded him of the drawing. He took it from his pocket and handed it to her. "Here. Oliver made this for you."

She unfolded the picture and studied it, a slow smile spreading across her beautiful face. "Is this the three of us?"

"Yeah. And that's the Statue of Liberty and Central Park and the Empire State Building," he said, pointing to the drawing.

"So coming to New York was Oliver's idea."

"I'd be lying if I said he didn't give me a little inspiration," Rhys admitted. "But the execution was all mine."

"You made quite an impression, that's for sure." She sank down onto the couch, the picture in one hand, her chardonnay in the other.

He sat next to her, close enough to feel the heat radiating off her skin but not so close they were touching. "A good one, I hope."

"I'm not sure what it all means."

She crossed her legs, and he tried to ignore the way her dress rode higher up her thighs. If there was ever a time for thinking with the head above his belt and not below, it was now.

"It means I need you. Oliver needs you. We want you back, Mallory."

"As your nanny?"

"No. That position has already been filled."

Her eyes widened. "It has?"

"Mm-hmm." He leaned back, casually stretching his arm across the back of the sofa. "And I think you'll agree I found the perfect person for the job."

"I don't know." Mallory took a sip of her wine. "She's got some pretty big shoes to fill."

"He."

"You hired a manny?"

"Not exactly."

"Okay, now I'm totally confused." Cute little furrows pleated her forehead, and he ached to take her in his arms and kiss them away. "Who is this caregiver extraordinaire?"

He pointed a thumb at his chest.

She stared at him blankly.

"You're looking at him," Rhys said.

Oliver's drawing fluttered to the floor. "You?"

"Why so surprised? You were the one who told me I needed to spend more time with my son."

"What about your work?"

He couldn't wait any longer. He had to touch her. He took the glass from her hand, put it next to his on the side table, and laced his fingers with hers. "I've got good people working for me. Collins is overdue for a promotion. I'll learn to delegate more. And what I can't delegate I can do when Oliver's asleep. Or in school."

"School?"

"I'm thinking Westchester County." Rhys turned her hand over and traced slow circles on her palm with his thumb. She rewarded him with a sharp intake of breath and a slight shiver. "Or maybe Fairfield, or somewhere on Long Island. Close to your parents but not too close. I was hoping you'd help me house hunt. I've been out of the tristate area for so long. I'm sure you know the real estate market better than I do."

"House hunt?" She frowned again, deepening the adorable creases in her brow. "What about Flamingo Key?"

"We'll spend summers on the island. School vacations

and holidays. But our home base will be here." Rhys dropped his arm from the back of the couch to her shoulders and clasped her hand tight. "I meant what I said, Mallory. You were right. I'm just starting to get to know my son. I don't want him to resent me as he grows up. It's time for us to rejoin the human race."

A tear slipped down her cheek to the corner of her tremulous smile. "You're doing the right thing."

"I'm not going to lie." His eyes caught hers and held. "It's not going to be easy. I've got a lot of baggage to sort through. I'm going to need some help."

"Of course. I'll do whatever I can."

"For starters, you can say you love me as much as I love you."

You could have driven a truck through the silence that followed his pronouncement. A wave of desperation washed over him.

"You heard me, right? I said I love you."

"Y-yes." Her chin dipped, and heat colored her cheeks.

He pulled her hand to his lips and peppered it with kisses. "I don't take those words lightly. I've only said them to one other woman. And I never thought I'd say them again. Then you crashed into my life like an asteroid and changed everything."

"An asteroid." She lifted her face. The start of a smile playing about the corners of her mouth and the light dancing in her eyes boosted his hopes, even though she hadn't said the words he longed to hear. Yet. "Sounds deadly."

"Not this one." He reached up to cup her cheek. "This one saved me."

"But…"

"No." He put a finger across her lips. "No buts."

"What if…?"

"No what-ifs either. We don't have to have all the answers

today. As long as we're willing to find them together."

She bit her lip and blinked back fresh tears. He mentally crossed his fingers that they were tears of happiness. Finally, after what seemed like an eternity but was probably only a few seconds, she brought her lips to his and kissed him, so soft and fleeting he almost thought he'd imagined it. "I'm game if you are."

"Oh, I'm game all right." To hell with soft and fleeting. He hauled her into his lap, cradling her.

"You're crazy." She clung to his shoulders, her nails biting into his skin through his thin shirt.

"So my elaborate plan to win you back worked?"

"I loved it." She pushed his collar aside and nuzzled his neck. "I love you."

Relief, sweet and sharp, flooded his heart. Words weren't enough to express the depth of his feelings, so he didn't bother to try, preferring to rely on the tried and true maxim that actions spoke louder. He parted her lips with his, slipping his tongue inside to find hers. They'd been apart less than a month, but they kissed like it had been years, locked together, their whole bodies involved. Mouths moving, chests melding, hands wandering, needy and desperate.

"Rhys," she protested when he let her up for air. She reached behind her to tug on the hem of her dress, which had risen almost to her waist in their frenzied groping. "My dress…"

"Is lovely." He smoothed a hand over the sleek curve of her ass, bare save for her lacy pink panties. "And it will look even better on the floor."

"Are you forgetting your son is downstairs? Along with my entire family?"

"What can I say?" He tucked a piece of hair that had escaped from her updo behind her ear. "When you do that thing with your tongue, I can't think about anything else."

"What thing with my tongue?" She batted her eyelashes, the picture of faux dewy-eyed innocence.

"You know full well. The thing where you trace my earlobe. It's very distracting."

"You're saying this is my fault?" She stood and adjusted her dress, the hint of laughter in her voice robbing her words of any sting.

"No." He rose to join her, making his own necessary adjustment to the crotch of his pants. "I'm saying we'll finish this later."

"I'm going to hold you to that." She stepped into her heels, which she must have kicked off during their make-out session. "But the logistics won't be easy. The reception's not over for a couple of hours, and my mother will kill me if I leave again. Oliver's going to be bouncing off the walls from all that chocolate. And I hope you have a hotel suite, because I've been staying with my sister and her husband and…"

He wrapped his arms around her waist and lifted her off her feet, silencing her with a kiss.

"Don't worry, sweetheart." He let her slide down his body slowly, intimately, feeling every inch or her with every inch of him. "We've got the rest of our lives to figure it out."

Epilogue

"All right. Time to wrap up." Mallory wiped her hands on her apron and surveyed her class of third and fourth graders at Pots 'n' Pans. The school had been filled almost to capacity since its grand opening six months ago, and today's collection of tiny chefs was no exception. Things were going so well, she was even considering adding a mommy and me class next term for toddlers. "Great work, everyone. Don't forget to clean up your stations before your parents get here. And take your cinnamon rolls home to share."

"What are we making next week?" Jayne, a redheaded spitfire who always sat in the front row, piped up.

"French toast on brioche bread with fresh strawberries and homemade whipped cream." Mallory rounded the room, making sure all ten kids in the small personalized class were following her instructions and using the safe kitchen practices she'd drilled into them in the first few sessions of the eight-week course.

"Sounds delicious." Rhys's voice made her head swivel toward the classroom door. He stood framed in the entryway, looking sexier than any man had a right to in slim-fit jeans and a crisp white button-down shirt rolled to his elbows. She put a hand to her throat. Even after almost a year together, he never ceased to make her breath come a little quicker and her heart beat a bit faster.

"Where's Oliver?" she asked, bending to help one of her increasing number of male students wrap his plate of cinnamon rolls. She'd always thought it strange that boys were steered away from the kitchen and toward more supposedly masculine pursuits like playing sports or building model rockets when so many of the top chefs were men. One of her prime objectives at Pots 'n' Pans was getting more boys to see that cooking was not only fun but unisex. "I thought we were taking him to karate together after I close up shop."

"Change of plans." Rhys moved to one side to let the first of the students out the door and into the waiting room, where Gwen, the newly hired receptionist, would make sure they were reunited with their family members. "He's with your parents. They're taking him to the dojo and then dinner at Dave & Buster's."

Mallory's mouth fell open. She was surprised it didn't hit the floor. "My mother agreed to set foot in an arcade?"

"Are you really that shocked?" Rhys stepped into the room as the last few students filed out. "Her soon-to-be grandson has her wrapped around his little finger."

She pulled out the chain from under her blouse and fingered the eight-carat emerald-cut diamond ring dangling from it. She wore it that way—close to her heart—when she was working. No use risking it getting caught in a mixer or winding up in one of her students' creations. "I guess I can't blame her. She'd pretty much given up on being a grandmother. Brooke and Eli aren't in any rush to have kids. And I…"

She broke off, looking down at the ring still in her hand.

Rhys put his arms around her, drawing her into his warmth, and brushed his lips against hers. "Don't. We talked about this. You know how I feel. I have everything I want with you and Oliver. And if we decide to expand our family, there are lots of ways to do that."

Like the Grinch at the end of the perennial Christmas cartoon, Mallory's heart swelled in her chest, threatening to burst free from her rib cage. She stood on tiptoe to wind her arms around Rhys's neck and threaded her fingers through his hair. "What did I do to deserve you?"

He lowered his head for another kiss, this one longer, more heated than the last. "Rescued me from a life of loneliness and solitude."

"That's right." She smiled up at him. "I did."

"Oliver's sleeping over at your parents' place, so we've got the whole night to ourselves." He ran a hand down her back, stopping just south of her waist. "Any ideas how we should spend it?"

"I've got a ton of stuff to do for the wedding." She fought for focus as his hand drifted farther south, cupping the curve of her ass. The big day was only a few weeks away, and she still had to finalize the seating arrangements, write her vows, get the head count to the caterer... "And I'm nowhere near ready to move. I haven't even started packing yet."

She and Rhys had agreed it wouldn't be appropriate for her to live with him and Oliver in the Oyster Bay home she'd helped them find and furnish until after the wedding. Her parents wanted her to move back into the guesthouse on their property, but Mallory had asserted her newfound independence and put her foot down, renting a cozy studio apartment in easy distance from Rhys and her new storefront in picturesque downtown Cold Spring Harbor.

"No." Rhys put a finger to her lips, quieting her. "No wedding stuff tonight. And no packing. Tonight is for us."

She kissed his palm and held it against her cheek. "What do you suggest?"

"I thought maybe dinner at L'Ecole. I've reserved the chef's table."

Mallory would have jumped for joy, but she didn't want Rhys to stop touching her. The heat of his palm on her face had tingles skipping down her spine to her nether regions. "Are you serious? It's almost impossible to get in there. And I've been dying to study Chef Ip's preparation and plating."

"So you've said. About a thousand times." His thumb stroked her lower lip, and the tingles turned to tremors. "Then I thought we'd follow that up with a walk on the beach and a night in my bed."

She sighed and relaxed into him. "That sounds perfect."

"It will be perfect when you're in my bed permanently."

"Soon." She kissed him and maneuvered out of his arms to do one last check of the room and grab her purse from the closet. "You know what they say. Patience is a virtue."

"A highly overrated virtue, if you ask me." He checked his watch. "Our reservation is in thirty minutes. We'd better get moving."

"There you go with that patience problem again," she teased, looping her purse over her shoulder and starting for the door. "Let me make sure Gwen is okay with locking up and we can head out."

He snagged her hand as she walked by and pulled her back to him.

"Hey," she squealed, laughing as she fell against him. His arms tightened around her again, keeping her upright. "I thought you were in a hurry."

"I am." His eyes sparkled as he lowered his smiling mouth to hers, stopping a fraction of an inch from her parted lips. "But no matter how busy we are, no matter how crazy our lives become, I don't want us to forget."

"Forget what?" she asked, the words coming out on a breathy whisper.

He closed the distance between them and their lips met, his soft and coaxing, fitting as naturally with hers as two puzzle pieces. When he was finished, he rested his forehead on hers, their noses touching, their eyes locked in a moment of awareness and understanding.

"That there's always time for this."

About the Author

Regina Kyle also writes for Harlequin Blaze. She is a 2018 and 2016 Booksellers' Best Award Winner (*Billionaire In Her Bed* and *Triple Dare*, both in the Erotic Romance category) and a 2017 National Readers' Choice Award Finalist (*Triple Score*–Erotic Romance). Regina knew she was destined to be an author when she won a writing contest at age ten with a touching tale about a squirrel and a nut pie. By day, she writes dry legal briefs, representing the state in criminal appeals. At night, she writes steamy romance with heart and humor. A lover of all things theatrical, Regina lives on the Connecticut coast with her husband, teenage daughter, and two melodramatic cats. When she's not writing, she's most likely singing, reading, cooking, or watching bad reality television. She's a member of Romance Writers of America and of her local RWA chapter.

Also by Regina Kyle...

THE BILLIONAIRE IN HER BED

Discover more category romance titles from Entangled Indulgence...

Giving Up the Boss

a *Billionaire's Second Chance* novel by Victoria Davies

Billionaire Jackson Sinclair wakes up in a hospital to a life he can't remember. The only person who feels familiar is Lori. The more he learns about his past, though, the more it disturbs him. He can't imagine why the lovely Lori put up with him. And she is lovely, as in, he can't stop thinking about her. But he has a company to save, and there's no time for that sort thing. Especially when it seems like his assistant is hiding something from him.

Scotland or Bust

a *Winning the Billionaire* novel by Kira Archer

After dumping her boyfriend, Nicole Franklin jumps on a plane and heads to Europe. Sure, money and a job would have been nice to line up first. Even a visa, for that matter. So now she has to play tour guide at an Outlander experience for the most obnoxious man on the planet. Until she stumbles into the wrong bed in the middle of the night and wakes up in Harrison's arms. Now his family thinks they're engaged, and the entire village is betting on how long before she runs for the hills.

BESTING THE BILLIONAIRE
a *Billionaire Bad Boys* novel by Alison Aimes

Billionaire Alexander Kazankov and Lily Bennett go toe-to-toe in an ugly, take no prisoners battle to prove they're the right choice to be CEO of the same company. All too soon playing dirty in the boardroom leads to playing even dirtier in the dark. It's destined to end in personal and professional disaster. So why the hell can't they stop?

THE PENTHOUSE PACT
a *Bachelor Pact* novel by Cathryn Fox

Billionaire software developer Parker Braxton knows everyone wants something from him. That's why he made a multi-million-dollar bachelor pact with his friends to never marry. But he never counted on running into, literally, the quiet but sensual Layla Fallon. Sparks fly. Hearts flutter. But falling for Layla could cost Parker more than just several million dollars.

Made in the USA
Columbia, SC
02 October 2018